Hi
I hope You Like the
Book!!! Thanks for
the hospitality!!!!

THE SIVILIN HUNTERS

jB

Jim Branger

CHAPTER ONE

Arak banked sharply and used his wings to pull with all of his strength. He looked back at the descending monster and realized that he'd been foolish to fly out over the Desowan wilderness. The sivilin was in a dive with wings swept back. With wings outspread he was sure they would span at least a hundred feet.

He'd been living in the eastern colony of Sagitar for seven years now. He'd met Enneka six summers before, and after many flights together along the front of the mountain range they had finally broken the rules and had succumbed to the lure of the dangerous wasteland. Only sivilin hunters with special training were allowed to fly out over the Desowan.

Enneka had finally coaxed Arak into soaring out over the arid wasteland with him and several mutual friends, and they weren't even carrying proper sivilin hunting gear. Today Arak and his friends were supposed to be hunting miktas or chura for meat in the foothills along the western slopes of the Sagitarian mountain range, not sivilin over the eastern Desowan and its myriad of canyons, intermittent streams and rocky mesas. Suddenly his life was in jeopardy. The youngsters weren't even allowed to hunt game at night yet without supervision, and in a way it was far less dangerous, as sivilin were seldom seen in the sky after dark.

Arak's crossbow was somewhat smaller than that of a sivilin hunter, and it was still slightly difficult for the young klute to pull and load the weapon while in flight. He was only sixteen, and wouldn't reach his full strength for a few more years. Sivilin hunters were required to pass certain tests, and the youngest hunters were all at least three years older than Arak or Enneka and they were armed with more formidable weapons.

Sivilin hunters were also trained in various multitasking aerobatic maneuvers involving complicated high wind velocities while firing arrows usually from an inverted falling or diving position while trying to maintain a safe distance from the sivilin. The long talon hook shaped non-retractable claws and fearsome fangs of the always aggressive and very dangerous flying predator had killed many klutes.

Sivilin hunters would try to shoot crossbow bolts into the soft neck, esophagus, or throat area of the huge flying nemesis. This was the only way to injure one of the creatures bad enough to cause death. Spearing the animals with any type of lance had proven to be too dangerous, and the scaly hides were almost impossible to penetrate from above anyway. Blinding the creatures had even been tried, but shooting them in the eyes was very difficult. To drop past the side of the monster in a position where an arrow could be delivered into an eye was also too close to one of the creature's wings, and any contact could cause serious injury to the klute.

Arak realized that his evasive maneuver had been successful, but he was still in grave danger. The sivilin was a couple hundred feet below him now, and it was definitely planning on making him its next meal. He performed another stunt by doing a quick half roll that put him into an inverted dive, then ascended to level flight at the bottom of the shallow dive. This maneuver gave him a lightning fast hundred and eighty degree change in direction, and the sivilin was too large to follow so quickly. Had it been slightly closer before he had sensed it Arak would already be dead.

A cold shiver ran down his spine, and he realized that he still wasn't safe when the giant lizard turned its head back while making a seventy or eighty-degree bank. Arak could hear the wind whistle past the sivilin's wings for a moment as they strained to cut through the air, then it shrieked at him. The close proximity allowed him to clearly see the intimidating black streaked face and long protective pointed horny growths protruding from above its golden eyes as it turned its head slightly sideways and looked directly at him. His four Sagitarian friends had all scattered, and the only one he could see at the moment was Rhee about five hundred yards to his right. She was flying as fast as she could in a northerly direction at a slightly lower altitude.

Arak pondered his situation while the monster maneuvered below him; shadowing his every move; stalking him. He knew he was wasting his time when he reached under the leather flap of his quiver and pulled out an arrow. He loaded his crossbow, but however futile it seemed, it was his only means of defense. Another shiver of panic shot through him when the thing began a slow deliberate climb while watching him intently almost as if toying with him as a much larger predator often does with its prey.

Arak tried to recall every memory he'd ever seen or heard about sivilin hunting, and he knew what to do, but he would have to time the move. He was in the worst possible situation for a winged hunter. Sivilin could fly and also gain altitude faster than any other creature on the planet, including a klute. The only way to elude one of the giant apex predators was to dive at terminal velocity. It took some time to reach the incredible speed, and had he tried to do the maneuver when he'd sensed the descending nemesis he probably would have ended up shredded by its massive jaws or been torn in half by its three foot long claws.

Thoughts flickered through his mind as he continued his climb. He wondered where his mother was. She'd gone out over the Desowan with a group of hunters two days before, and had left him with his friends in the Sagitarian academy learning boring basic imaging skills of which he was already prolific. He recalled Miz's warning words of wisdom before her departure.

"Make sure you put some smoked jerky and lystroroot in your pack if you go out hunting with your friends. And be sure you follow your instructor's advice to perfection whenever you practice blindfolded imaging descents into Sagitar."

His father was one of the best sivilin hunters from Sagitar, perhaps the whole delta, and unlike most individuals his age, Arak had seen many shared neural images and vivid first hand memories of aerial combat with the creatures. A friend of his father's had projected first hand memories at a signal fire in the Glass Canyon the previous fall, and Arak had been lucky enough to witness them after preparing the fire below a low murky cloud ceiling. Most disciples of the klute academies weren't allowed to witness combat memories or graphic neural images until they'd graduated or finished classes giving them professional tasks within the colonies, but there were so many exceptions with escalating sivilin numbers, that excluding the very young, the rule was just becoming a formality, and not followed strictly.

Arak would try to imitate one of the visions he'd witnessed at the signal fire. If he failed he would be killed. He continued his slow climb, and tried to remain as calm as possible while glancing behind and below. The large predator began to close in. The thing had a wingspan of well over a hundred feet; almost five times that of Arak's. He would have to time his move perfectly.

When the sivilin was about fifty yards behind him and still twenty or thirty yards below he suddenly reversed direction again and dove directly toward it. The giant flying lizard was caught off guard, and when it raised its head and opened its saber-toothed maw Arak was safely diving toward the end of its tail. He aimed at the creature's head and pulled the trigger of his crossbow as he plummeted past, then with tightly folded wings he plunged headfirst toward the semi-arid, scrubby pine forest far below. The stench of the giant reptilian creature permeated the air around him for a moment in the close quarters. Arak had heard of the unpleasant odor associated with the sivilin, but he'd never been within a couple miles of one until now. He'd actually only seen a few sivilin alive in his life.

He was at about three quarters timberline or seven thousand feet when he started the descent, and the sivilin was swift to follow, but not quick enough. The young klute reached terminal velocity with the long fangs and hooked claws of the shrieking monster safely behind.

He was still about a thousand feet above the ground when the sivilin finally began to pull out of its dive, but it continued circling downward, and Arak just then realized how well it blended into the backdrop of sparsely clouded sky. The light grey, green, and cerulean blue splotched underside of the creature made it appear almost invisible from below.

He began unfolding his wings to slow his descent while looking for a suitable hiding place, and decided the taller trees of a patchy deciduous and pine forest near a rocky promontory to his south looked the best. There was a small intermittent stream carving its way past the little square butte, and he banked in the general direction while still at a speed that was almost beyond the stress limitations of the flexible bones in his wings. When he was safely in the forest below the sparse upper canopy of foliage he chose a tall leafy tree and an easily accessible branch.

He stood motionless against the five foot diameter tree trunk, and watched the sivilin circle rapidly downward. The giant flying lizard leveled off about three hundred feet above the ground and began searching aimlessly for the klute, but it soon realized that it was wasting its time or decided to go after easier prey elsewhere. Arak was sweating, which was very unusual for a klute, and trembling slightly when the thing finally flew off toward the north. He didn't have to wait long before it was out of sight.

Sivilin encounters were occurring daily over the Desowan, and even sometimes west of the mountains. There seemed to be no end to the flying scourge, and over the past five years the entire klute population of the delta and Moktaw Islands had actually slightly declined. It seemed that no matter how many sivilin were killed or driven off more appeared from some unknown source.

There was no record of such a vicious cycle in any of the klute's history scrolls, but there were stories and rumors from an ancient time that told of a period when sivilin dominated the skies. In the recorded past sightings and encounters with the giant lizards definitely peaked at certain intervals, but they'd always looked elsewhere for prey after continual harassment by the klutes.

With the present day escalation crossbow bolts didn't seem to be a strong enough deterrent, but precise maneuvers and precision accuracy with the handmade weapons was their only means of defense. Firing thick shafted arrows into the throat and neck area while plunging past and in front of the sivilin was the preferred method. A few well placed crossbow bolts could penetrate the throat and esophagus causing a lingering death, or even slice through the jugular vein or one of the neck arteries causing a quicker demise.

If they couldn't be stopped the sivilin would make short work of the mikta and chura populations west of the Sagitarian range, and the klutes would all have to look elsewhere for wild game. Perhaps only the Mocktaw Islands would be a safe haven, but in the past year sivilin had even been sighted far out over the sea. The cold rainy forested mountains to the north and west might offer protection, but sivilin had also been seen north of the delta many times. The winged race wasn't fond of a sea supporting diet, but it had saved them in the past when a severe frigid climate change had occurred over the delta.

Arak's first nine years had been spent in the Glass canyon academy of the coastal range, but the entire colony had since moved to Sagitar to help repel the encroaching sivilin. For several years the giant flying scourge had pulled back, but over the past two years they'd been advancing upon the delta in numbers never before seen or recorded in even the most ancient scrolls or archives of the winged race.

Arak stood safely on a branch of the tall coniferous tree and closed his keen eyes. They were dark yellow eyes with brown and blue streaks or flecks scattered throughout both irises. He could magnify his vision perfectly for a few seconds; up to almost five times normal.

His wings were folded tightly. The hollow flexible bones and thin elastic, regenerative skin of his wings took up very little space behind him. He searched the telepathic rifts for images, and could sense someone right away. He tried to connect by putting all thoughts from his mind while concentrating on the neural signal. He steadied a tiny spark in the center of his vision, and suddenly the images began to take form. It was Shandra. She was out of danger somewhere far above and slightly to the west. He immediately opened his eyes and sent back images of his position within the tall pines while sensing a link from Enneka, and perhaps another from Rhee or Dulles. He was glad all of the members of their hunting party were ok. Dulles was from the southern klute colony of Taro, and like Arak his family had relocated a few years earlier for sivilin hunting.

Unfortunately his father had been killed over the Desowan since then.,

Except for perhaps Arak, the young klutes were all still just below the final stages of heightened neural ascension, but Arak had shown remarkable abilities at the age of six and had even passed his final solo beyond horizon hunting exercises at the young age of nine. The group was able to home in on his strong neural link, and within a few minutes they were all standing in the forest below.

"It's gone off to the east." Said Enneka as he touched down. He was as tall as Arak, a few inches under six feet, and the hair covering the top of his head had recently been cropped around ears that slanted back against the side of his head. Klutes could move and rotate their slightly pointed ears a tiny bit, and were able to use the trait to enhance their facial expressions in some instances. Enneka's dark grey eyes almost seemed to smolder at times giving him a distinguished sense of intelligence, and he usually led the class hunting expeditions.

The fresh green grass coming up through the pine needled floor of the partially shaded clearing exuded pleasant springtime aromas, and Arak began to calm down. The encounter had been the most intense experience of his life.

"It almost had you." Rhee looked at him with a horrified expression. "I could even see it turning its head watching you, stalking you." She was about five foot seven, and had a wingspan close to twenty feet when her wings were spread. Her eyes were light brown, about the same color as her long hair. It had been tied in a couple of knots on top of her head. The rest of the sparse hair on her exposed arms and lower legs was also very light brown, almost translucent, and aside from being kind of chubby she was attractive.

"We shouldn't be out here." Answered Arak. "The rules of the colony have been passed down for an obvious reason." Then he laughed almost out of control. "I think I might have hit it in the side of the head with an arrow."

He'd stopped worrying about his father for the moment, and his laughter was contagious. Soon all five of the young klutes were laughing off their apprehension. The brief encounter had taken the young group of students into another world. The world of sivilin hunters. It was a dangerous place with restricted image sharing. Rhee's mother had been killed, Dulles's father had also been killed, and Arak's father was missing. The neural images of Rhee's mother's demise were restricted; so graphic that no children and only certain individuals within private circles were allowed to witness them. There were many telepathic images and visions that were supposed to be censored within the colony, but it was difficult to police the rule.

"We need to go higher is all." Said Enneka as he wiped uncontrollable tears of laughter from his face. "That thing was huge!! It must have been way above timberline or we would have seen it."

"The upper air flow is almost always from the east if we go any higher." Arak was suddenly serious as if thinking. "Unless there's a big storm off of the west coast, but we could go to timberline and a half on the way home the next time we come out here."

"Well who did see it first?" Asked Shandra. "Everyone seemed to panic at the same time; I just followed Dulles. I didn't even know it was around till it circled below us, or below Arak. It smelled like something that has been dead for a week or so."

Shandra was the only one in the group that was from the coastal colony, and she'd known Arak since the two of them had been able to speak. She was also about five foot seven and her eyes were a light shade of green with yellow and brown flecks. Her light brown hair was tied in a braid and lay in front of her shoulder. She was also very attractive, stunning when she was dressed for celebrations or image sharings.

"I heard the wind over its wings when it pulled out of its dive. I guess it was just spreading them." Arak glanced at Shandra. "When I looked back I couldn't believe my eyes. I think everyone else heard it at about the same time. If I hadn't seen it when I did I would be dead right now. The talons only missed me by a couple of feet. Did anybody hear me yell?"

"Yes. I heard you. We were lucky." Enneka looked at him. "We'd better keep this a secret, or Magahila will make us do blindfolded maneuvers into the Sagitarian gorge for a week in gusty weather, or worse yet. She might make us wash the dishes and serve the first three classes in the academy for a week or two."

Shandra had removed her small pack or knapsack, and she was rummaging inside for a snack of chalow cheese or jerky.

She glanced up momentarily. "Magahila is kind of mean sometimes. Duroon is too. He'll make us clean the chalow pens and herd them on the steppes for the rest of the summer if he finds out we've been over the Desowan. Magahila caught your cousin Starral sneaking wine from a table at one of the killing celebrations last year and Orem made her stay inside of the imaging room during all of the morning, afternoon, and even our lunch breaks for almost a month."

"Yeah, I know" Answered Enneka. "Starral said the wine tasted very nice though; She hated washing the dishes in the academy the most, and of course cleaning the latrines."

Rhee looked around cautiously at their surroundings and suddenly stooped to pick some mushrooms that she knew were edible. Watching

Shandra snack on cheese was making her hungry. Even though she was kind of chubby she had very strong wings and was always able to keep up with the rest of the group.

Rhee poured water from her flask on one of the toadstools and washed it carefully. She spoke while laughing quietly. "When Jenga and his family visited from Taro last winter he got caught drinking brandy at the hibernation feast. His parents grounded him for their entire stay at Magahila's request, and he had to clean the chalo pens as part of his punishment too. I can't really believe I'm standing here in the Desowan right now."

"The rules are made for a reason." Arak glanced up at the sky and squinted. "If scroll and imaging lessons weren't so boring I would follow them perfectly. I've never had a feeling like that. It seemed like it was looking right into my eyes, maybe even with enhanced vision."

Dulles stretched his wings beneath a tall tree about fifteen feet from Arak and he turned toward Enneka with a worried look.

"Well." He said. "We aren't allowed to hunt at night so we are going to see a few sivilin. It's going to get dark in about six hours; we'd better get going if we want to find miktas or get some images of Moon Creek for Magahila from the other side of the divide."

The youngster had recently moved with his family from the Taro colony, and like many of the southern colony klutes he had blue eyes and a slightly lighter shade of hair. He was about the same height as Shandra.

The small group of students all knew they would be in trouble if they didn't make it back to Sagitar by dark. Whether or not they were successful hunting later in the day would be immaterial in all three of their imaging instructor's eyes, but if they weren't back in the academy by dark they would be punished in trivial ways, and parents that were home would be very worried and disappointed. They would have to go back over the divide so they could gain some fresh neural images of hunting grounds west or north of Sagitar.

They'd all removed their packs, so they began slinging them onto their shoulders and between wings while adjusting and tying the straps to assure comfortable flight. Arak's pack needed some adjustment after his terminal dive, but Shandra helped him tighten the center straps slightly before they began walking toward a wide clearing about a hundred yards to the southeast. Soon they were all airborne, and they headed back toward the nearby mountains. The winds remained light offering them little resistance and the group flew low sometimes skimming the treetops until they began their ascent over the Sagitarian divide. Flying low was dangerous, and they constantly had to be vigilant from an attack from above, but they would be able to hide very swiftly if need be.

Arak breathed a sigh of relief when they rose above the mountain pass north of Thunder mountain. They began a slow effortless glide over the familiar bare rocky sometimes vertical terrain below and to the west. The five of them stayed slightly above timberline and began searching clearings and openings in the forested valleys west of the Sagitarian River, but were disappointed with the absence of miktas or chura. There were several species of each residing on the delta. Some as small as deer, others as large as buffalo or moose. It was too warm, and the small herds of herbivores would probably remain hidden or bedded down in the shade until dusk. Sivilin had also thinned the larger herds close to the mountains, so the group wasn't surprised.

They continued over the pass west of the colony between Froze to Death and Tempest mountains, and flew onward toward Moon creek. There was no game to be found so they began a slow circumventing arc to the south while following the stream.

Arak suddenly felt a tingling sensation in the back of his head and closed his eyes while sustaining a stable glide. He concentrated on the tiny spark, and the images exploded into view. It was someone he didn't know, probably one of the scouts that flew out of the colony daily, or maybe someone from one of the sivilin hunting packs. He doubted if anyone was hunting sivilin west of the mountains, and tried to get a directional singularity. He concentrated on the link trying to center it in his vision while using the grueling technique that Orem had taken hours and even years to drill into his complex synapses. A few seconds later he opened his eyes and saw that his direction had changed ninety degrees.

"What are you doing?" asked Enneka who had been following close behind. "Sagitar is this way."

"Someone is coming from the west." Arak swiveled his head and glanced back at him. "I think it's one of the scouts."

"Maybe they have spotted some game somewhere." Said Shandra as she pulled up alongside the other two.

Arak centered the singularity again and banked slightly to the south. A few minutes later they spotted the lone scout. They joined up with her and found that she hadn't seen any game for three hours glide but there was a chura herd north of the wind river outpost. The scout's name was Vallah.

Rhee, Enneka and Dulles all knew her family but though Arak had heard of her he'd never met her in person. She was one of about a dozen of the free ranging scouts that inhabited Sagitar, and she had been out over the Desowan many times.

They decided to return to Sagitar while zig zagging south over several popular hunting locations. Vallah had been flying from the northwest since sunrise, and she made a beeline for the colony. Mount Sagitar rose from the skyline to their left, higher than most of the surrounding peaks that were all above timberline, and she would be there in about an hour and a half with the help of a slightly lower eastward air flow. There was Thunder mountain just to the left of Sagitar, and Froze to Death was also north with mount Tempest. Of the higher peaks Pyramid and the double summit of Mawl mountain were visible to the south.

Enneka knew every nook and cranny of the area surrounding the colony for a half day's glide, and they finally spotted a small herd of miktas that was beginning to stray from a tangled grove of saplings at the bottom of a giant coulee that drained into one of the unnamed canyons of the Sagitarian river.

They were on their way home and glacial moraine lay scattered around the area deposited by ice centuries before. Some of the smooth rounded stones, or erratics, towered twenty feet from the thin sandy topsoil of the rugged carved Sagitarian foothills. It was almost dusk and there was only one young buck with the herd, so they headed for the city empty handed.

Sagitarian academic instructors Magahila, and Duroon were both in the spacious student cavern when they returned, and Orem was giving gliding lessons from an adjoining room to a group of younger children. Arak's hunting group was awaiting graduation in a class of about fifteen depending on visitors from the other klute colonies, and all five of them were in their last year of image processing. The instructors were disappointed with the results of the hunt, but not surprised. Students were usually restricted to half a day's glide from the academy, and returned with no game most of the time.

"We might have to extend your hunting grounds." Said Duroon with a smile as they all folded their wings. His short dark hair was streaked with grey and his blue eyes had a twinkle. "You have all ascended to the final level easily, and we've expanded hunting territories for the graduating class many times."

Enneka and Arak glanced at each other, and they both knew their instructors were suspicious.

"There's nothing close anymore." Said Enneka. "We've searched every creek, drainage, and crevasse within a half day's glide. We haven't seen any herds with more than one buck anywhere."

Magahila looked up from her work. She was weaving a large lightweight basket from thin long stemmed blades of a tough grass found near the southern Taro colony. "We'll talk to Orem when he's finished and see if you can go toward the Wind River on your next hunt, maybe spend a night out." Her yellow eyes, pointy nose, close cropped hair, and long bony fingers gave her a sinister appearance that she knew how to take advantage of at certain times.

Enneka quickly shared some images of their flight to the west showing the small group gliding over Moon creek, and they departed for their homes. Arak wondered if Duroon could see past the main images into some of Enneka's hidden memories. The instructors were obviously suspicious of their travels, but they'd had many graduation classes to deal with, and he realized that sometimes students had been over the Desowan in the past. A few had even been killed.

The next day the small class of five studied some of the writing and arithmetic scrolls that had been handed down by the klute race. The age of the five students was all about the same; within a year, but they were actually only half of their original class. There were six other students in the same age group, but due to the more complex lessons the older classes were always split in two.

Sagitar had a lot of visitors, especially in the summer, and visiting students were usually put into a separate group. Arak, Enneka, Dulles, Shandra, and Rhee were in Arak's class. Their group was slightly ahead of the other six, but their other classmates were very competitive. A female led the second group. Her name was Tillery and she could memorize lessons much faster than anyone else in any of the upper classes. She was already projecting images from way beyond the line of sight of horizon, and she could pull a fairly strong crossbow. There was also Kenivel. He was almost as good as Tillery when it came to sending or receiving images.

Contests between the two halves of the class were very intense, but Arak and Enneka's group usually edged out the other. One of the students in Tillary's group was very tall and already had a wingspan of twenty five feet, but he was kind of clumsy when it came to acrobatics or sporadic combined jumping, running, and flying exercises. Ormsby tried hard but he was always behind when it came to coordinated maneuvers. Rhee was also having trouble in this category. Swope, Saran, and Yaz were all tough to beat at any game of skill involving imaging or memory lessons. Yaz was perhaps the best bowshot of all eleven students, but her crossbow was a little bit weaker than any of the male students, and though not a very good weapon for a big chura bull, she could hit a mikta behind the shoulder at over a hundred paces every time.

Calisthenics and pull ups on an old pole crossbar set within the academy were done a few times a week by most students to increase muscle mass, and they were all able to pull a very dangerous crossbow and load it with an arrow. Some had trouble loading their bows while doing acrobatic maneuvers of any kind, but they were all getting better with practice.

Klutes were only given a first name at birth, and to prevent inbreeding each family simply kept a numbered scroll with the family tree dating back three or four generations. This wasn't followed very closely, but first or second cousins never mated. The klutes knew that inbreeding caused health problems and even birth defects of certain kinds.

Orem was supreme in the Glass Canyon colony, and he was teaching them how to tell time a little more accurately at night by looking at the stars. Some of them moved and some didn't, and it had been confusing for them when they were first learning. Even Arak had trouble remembering which stars rose with the sunset during different seasons or for different years, and there were also moon cycles to memorize.

The smaller red moon circled the planet almost twice as slow as the bright moon, but not quite, so it was a cycle that had to be memorized. The klutes liked hunting during the evenings when only the red moon was present in either a waxing or waning stage of half or more, but could kill efficiently in any night or day situation or weather. It offered them perfect lighting for hunting in this stage, and kept them completely cloaked from their prey. It also kept them hidden from the landwalkers that occupied the delta to the west of Sagitar.

The klutes had studied the landwalkers for many generations and had found them kind of boring and harmless. The race of humans had weapons and crafts similar to the klutes, and even planted vast fields of crops, but they were restricted to traveling by riding animals, walking, or taking water craft of various types. They were completely left alone, and almost ignorant of the flying klutes, or the encroaching sivilin. The northern race of landwalkers was barbaric and sometimes attacked the southern race for no reason that the klutes could discern, but they were still left alone in their endeavors.

The klutes had some gardens near their caves and cliff dwellings but didn't plant grains. Just various vegetables, spices, and wild fruits or fruit trees.

Arak could add and subtract numbers in his head, and he'd mastered all of the reading symbols and signs, but he still stayed in class with his friends and practiced skills that had been mostly outdated generations before his time due to increased image sharing capabilities. His parents had always insisted that he learn a brief history of the race, but he wasn't sure to what purpose it served, and adding and subtracting numbers was a complete waste of time as far as he was concerned. He'd also been fully capable of leaving a written message for someone for several years.

Arak wasn't fond of the imaging games and could care less if someone else could send numbered neural signals better than him to win a boring contest. The only imaging contests or games that he enjoyed involved directional flying while searching for a hidden partner or partners; usually in the darkness of a moonless night. Marksmanship contests were his favorite. Like most klutes his age he just wanted to soar on thermals and hunt or explore.

Their expedition over the Desowan went unnoticed and no one mentioned it, not even Rhee who was notorious for gossiping to her friends within or out of the academy. After a blindfolded imaging descent by each of them into the gorge just south of the klute city the class was dismissed for the day.

After a dip in the hot spring up behind the main cavern Arak and Shandra spent the evening with Arak's mother. Miz had just returned from sivilin hunting over the Desowan. She'd prepared dinner for them, and was interested in the student's progress with beyond line of sight imaging. She wasn't surprised at the failed hunting expeditions over the past few weeks. Chura stew simmered in the kitchen.

The fresh meat had been given to them from friends that had hunted far to the southwest the day before. They'd found a nice herd of the large cloven hooved quadrapeds almost halfway to the Baden river colony. In fact it was on the fringes of the southern colony's hunting grounds. In previous years someone from the Baden river colony might complain, but with the impending sivilin invasion it was irrelevant. The spiced chura stew was laden with vegetables and lystoroot, and Arak started his first bowl as soon as he entered the family dwelling.

"Are you going hunting again tomorrow?" asked Miz, her ears twitched slightly awaiting his answer. Her light hair was braided into double braids that hung in front of her shoulders.

"Probably." Answered Arak. "We just did boring scrolls and imaging today. A couple blindfolded descents, but even Shandra is getting so she can get all the way down to a hundred feet without peeking."

"I finally made it all of the way down into the gorge blindfolded with no problem." Shandra scooped a nice chunk of lystoroot. Her wooden spoon was tipped with an intimidating double pronged fork. "Some of the Taro students were here again today, and they had trouble making it down in the gusts and thermals. They don't have mountains near as high as ours to practice in."

Arak laughed. "I've been wondering when you were going to get enough nerve not to peek." He'd been dropping toward a neural signal from Orem for almost two years; sometimes through a cloud ceiling that was only a couple hundred feet above the ground. "I think only one of the Taro class made it down without raising their blindfolds. They sure think they are hot stuff. Mik can shoot a bow as good as me, but maybe only on the ground."

Shandra looked at him and laughed. "He was sure surprised when you beat him in the marksmanship contest last week. He's supposed to be the best young bow shot in the delta according to Orem."

"He's good." Arak laughed. "If it hadn't been for a gust of wind that blew through he would have tied me with the last shot. I'm sure glad you made it down into the gorge without looking this afternoon."

It was nothing compared to what we were doing a couple of days ago." She speared another chunk of lystroot malevolently with her fork.

"What sort of maneuvers did Orem have you doing?" Miz had a worried look on her face, and her green eyes scrutinized Shandra.

Shandra realized that she'd made a mistake, and glanced toward Arak for help.

"Oh nothing." He scooped stew from his bowl with a piece of rare hard toasted bread that had been brought from the Taro colony. "We dove into some thick trees at a dangerous speed the other day. Nothing that serious."

He glanced at Shandra and grinned sensing her immediate relief. They didn't want anyone to know about their journey into the Desowan, not even Miz.

"Who was in charge?" Miz was curious, but not surprised. Young klutes seemed to like challenging tasks, and sometimes they ended up dead or seriously injured. It was the reason strict rules had been made and passed down by the race over the generations.

"We were just hunting." Said Arak with a shrug. "I guess I was in charge; sort of anyway. Enneka likes to be the prime hunter though. He knows all of the best spots so we always follow him."

Miz walked to the cave entrance and unfurled her wings partially until the tips just touched the floor. She looked out at the sunset and closed her eyes. She'd been hopelessly searching the rifts for weeks. Cin had disappeared somewhere over the Northern Desowan, probably north of the Serlian mountains while scouting alone almost two months ago, and every evening she would check for a neural signal.

"I scanned the horizon from way above timberline this morning." Said Arak. "I didn't feel a thing, not even a stirring."

Miz turned and looked at the floor. A prime zinda hide lay outstretched, the clean white tanned fur was immaculate. Cin had killed it in the granite canyons east of the Glass canyon colony three years previous during midwinter.

Cin had disappeared while scouting somewhere over the northern Desowan weeks ago. Several scouts had died over the past few years, but the entire continent had been explored and mapped in more detail than ever before; even the windy desolate islands of the arctic, and the far eastern seaboard beyond the high mountain ranges that loomed to the east of the maze of grassy canyons, mesas and eroded hills of the sivilin's favored Desowan. No one had ever returned from a long distance flight over the polar ice cap, and except for the Mocktaw Islands, flights far out to sea in any direction usually ended up the same way.

Cin was a remarkable individual with perhaps higher than average intelligence, and he'd already explored the arctic twice. He said that he might try to be the first klute to cross the arctic sea and bring back images of the islands and whatever lay beyond the polar ice.

He had been seriously injured twice while attacking the enormous flying reptiles, but he'd been performing ill-advised insane attacks with a spear. The last attack caused him to be grounded for almost six months with a damaged wing, but he'd actually killed one of the sivilin single-handedly with a specially crafted lance. He'd improved his design a couple of times, and one of his spears even had hand grips, but it was almost impossible to drive the weapon into a sivilin's back through the bony plates and scales far enough to cause serious injury. There were records of only one other sivilin hunter that had ever tried the same insane method of attack with no success, and he had died while attempting the feat. There were enough faded images of the graphic encounter to discourage most others. The fatality had kindled a massive image sharing within the Sagitarian amphitheater with a crowd of almost five hundred. Savant was supreme, and along with the elders present in the colony they deemed the act too dangerous. They highly discouraged anyone else to even try a similar attack of any kind.

Miz was still standing by the doorway and gazing out over the valley. "I'm sure your father is fine." She said quietly. "He's been gone for long periods before, and he said this trip would be his and Dramadar's longest ever. Savant wanted them to scout the northern coastline and mountains if possible. He said he was going to go over the Serlian mountains; maybe all of the way to the Arctic sea. He's been close to there before. There are huge limestone ridge outcroppings all along the northern fringes and tundras, and it's been one of his goals to even try crossing the north sea someday. The sivilin are reproducing too fast in the Desowan or others are coming from somewhere else. When Dramadar turned back he said that he and your father were in sight of the northern range."

Arak looked at the prime zinda hide. It was one of his father's most prized possessions. The old cat had been huge, with very unusual markings; almost a trophy of sorts. Half of the tail, one of the front paws and the ears were black. There was also a dark oblong diamond shaped patch on the chest that had been split with the skinning of the animal. "What are the landwalkers up to?" He asked his mother.

Miz creased her forehead in thought. "Hunters from down south have found nothing new. The strange landwalkers from the northern shoreline are mostly gone from the delta, and they have taken their sailing ships back to their villages with them. I think the sivilin have only attacked their domesticated herds a couple of times but because of our interference they haven't killed many. The landwalkers are aware of the sivilin now; I think the first of their hunters sighted one a couple of months ago, somewhere north of their largest inland city."

Arak didn't answer. He wasn't interested in the landwalkers. To him they were just boring. It took the race of humans days to journey distances that he could travel in several hours if the wind was in his favor. He doubted if they could even send or receive images, but it was rumored that some could.

Dramdar had accompanied Cin from Sagitar into the northern region, and had returned alone less than a week ago. He said the northern skies were fairly clear of sivilin, but they had seen a few grazing the grass and mossy permafrost tundra south of the

Serlian mountains. Dramadar said Cin was planning to continue onward for a few days; or a maybe a week at the most when they split up.

Scouting or sivilin hunting to the north was usually considered a waste of time, but Savant and his tiny Sagitarian counsel had suggested and persuaded the expedition to the partially unexplored region. Cin had already surpassed his services as a sivilin hunter ten-fold, and some of his injuries were still slightly hindering him. He'd welcomed the mission as a mild excursion from the Desowan.

The small family of three had a made a pact the year before, and if any of them were ever missing or maybe presumed dead they would continue on with their lives as if nothing had happened. None of them would do anything foolish such as aimlessly going off searching for another family member alone, and Arak and Miz would stick to the pact. When someone was missing for more than six months or so the colony would simply hold an image sharing celebration for the missing individual.

Enneka led the way with Arak and Shandra just below. Dulles, and Rhee soared another weak thermal just to the north, and the summit of Mount Sagitar loomed majestically off to the east, its glaciers and snow streaked summits glowing brightly along with the colorful wispy clouds of the dawning sun. Searchlight rays rose between the clouds into the dark blue heavens. The early morning air was still calm and cold, and they were forced to use their wings until they finally reached timberline. The four of them followed Enneka as he flew west toward Moon Creek and their depleted hunting grounds. The sun felt good as Arak worked to maintain a westward flight with his friends.

Klutes could withstand cold temperatures with very little discomfort for hours at a time due to a spleen like organ that provided hyperoxygenated blood. The organ could even regulate their body temperatures slightly, and also allow them to soar above the troposphere where there was almost no air for several hours at a time.

As the weeks had progressed the five students had hunted farther and farther from Sagitar. Usually they came back empty handed, but sometimes they would find a mikta herd with more than two bucks and they would kill one. The sivilin had killed most of the chura on the northern delta. Sometimes they would even see one of the flying creatures in the distance, but they always stayed away from them.

They were still flying against a weak low westward headwind and were about three hours glide beyond Moon Creek. They had only sighted two bands of miktas and a pair of mountain chura. One of the chura had antlers but it was a young bull. Both of the mikta herds were supporting lone bucks so they left them alone as they did the chura. Hunters were flying beyond the Wind River outpost daily so there was no need to kill animals in small herds close to home.

As usual the five of them flew in a vee formation to conserve energy due to wind resistance. This also made it easier to keep everyone in sight. They made a slow turn to the north and began circling back toward the Sagitarian range. Shandra spotted sivilin at about the same time as Arak, and her loud whistle alerted the rest. She was pointing toward the mountains, and though the outlines were faint, two sivilin could be seen against the snowfields and they weren't that far away.

"Let's drop and land in the forest before they see us." Shandra spoke loud enough for all of them to hear.

"I'm with you." Rhee answered with a frightened tone of conviction in her voice. Her cheeks were slightly pink in the cool air.

"Wait a minute." Said Enneka. "We're above them and they haven't seen us." He banked until he was on a flight path that would intersect that of the two sivilin and he laughed. "Let's try put some arrows into them. It will be good practice."

Arak looked at his friend. "Are you serious? You're crazy."

"Hah." Dulles also laughed as he drifted up alongside. "Of course he's not serious. Look they're turning away from us!"

"The forest is thick out here. Let's see if we can catch them." Enneka glanced around at the rest of them. "Unless you're afraid."

"I'm not going." Said Rhee, but when she looked at Shandra for reassurance she was disappointed not to find it.

"I guess we don't have to go with them." Shandra looked at her. "But I don't' think it's as dangerous as the elders say."

Surviving the close up encounter a couple of weeks before with no problem had sparked a deep spirit of adventure within all of their mindsets, and even though some of the teenagers had lost family members they were suddenly eager to toy with the unknown and forbidden dangers of sivilin hunting.

"Hunting miktas is boring." Said Arak. "I think I'll go with Enneka and practice falling in front of them. I dropped away from that one over the Desowan with no problem as soon as I tucked my wings. The forest is thicker out here and we can hide easy enough. We don't all have to go though."

Rhee grimaced and looked at Arak. "You know how Duroon discourages us from thrill seeking. He doesn't even want us to go near a dust devil." She was just to his left and had pulled up alongside. "And Orem said to stay away from them."

"Yeah, I know." Answered Arak. He knew about Rhee's mother's death and had seen the images. "They're overprotective though. Your mother never had a chance. The sivilin came out of a cloud from above her. We have the advantage here. We'll make sure we stay out in front far enough like your father showed us when we shot at the targets last fall." He turned his head and glanced back at Shandra as the five of them banked slightly to follow the sivilin.

Dulles appeared for a moment as if he was reluctant, then he pulled his crossbow around on its leather sling so he could cock it. "I was hoping you weren't serious, but I'd like to make amends for my father." He said. "I'll go as long as nobody finks on us. I don't like being punished by Duroon or Magahila. Or any of the elders.

"You really want to dive on two of them?" Arak was still dubious as he flew up beside Enneka and pulled an arrow from his quiver.

"Might as well." Enneka answered grimly. "We've seen enough images, and like you said; we were able to get away from that one over the Desowan. Let's just make sure we're far enough ahead of them when we drop past like Rhee said. We can hide in the forest below easy enough. It's not like the wasteland."

All five of them decided to stick together and loose a few arrows. They slowly began to close in on the sivilin. They were a couple thousand feet above timberline, and were gaining on the giant flying lizards with a rare stream of air from the northwest at the higher altitude. Soon they were directly above the two giant flying lizards. The sivilin had their attention focused on the forest below when the klutes began a silent descent. Arak, Shandra, and Rhee would shoot at the one on the left, and Enneka and Dulles would loose crossbow bolts at the one on the right.

The sivilin were at about three quarters timberline or seventy-five hundred feet above sea level, and Arak and his four Sagitarian friends were at about twelve thousand feet when they broke one of the most serious rules of engagement set down by the klute race. It prohibited students or inexperienced hunters from attacking or approaching a sivilin in any way.

Arak was on the left with Shandra and Rhee to his right. Dulles and Enneka were about fifty yards to the north of Rhee as they started the inverted dive. They fell headfirst past the two giant lizards at a speed somewhere around a fourth terminal velocity and fired their crossbows.

Right away Arak knew they were falling too fast for his aim, and he watched his arrow fly harmlessly low penetrating only a couple inches into the scaly skin of the monster's chest between its slender front legs. The sivilin were startled and they both quickly raised their heads. Arak couldn't help noticing the huge claws or talons as he plunged past. He realized that his practice and expertise when falling and

shooting targets with his father along the sheer obsidian cliffs of the glass canyons and the cliffs north
of mount Sagitar might help him in the long run,
but he wished the academy would let them practice
more often.

Orem and the other instructors still balked when
the students wanted to perform aerial maneuvers
combined with archery, and usually made a family member accompany any students that wished to
practice. It was dangerous, and the best vertical cliffs
high enough for the stunts were over a half hour's
glide north of mount Sagitar. The wind was usually blowing erratically along the gigantic northern
rims, and students were discouraged from taking
certain aerial risks. Orem always laughed and said
they would have plenty of time to practice advanced
maneuvers after they'd graduated and could hopefully use a full sized bow.

Many of the Sagitarian klutes would practice dil-
igently right before the annual games of skill that
had just recently been reintroduced. The games had
been moved from Taro to Sagitar due to the sivilin
encroachment over the past four years. The inverted
maneuvers and contests along the two thousand foot
rims were restricted to certain weather conditions
and only the most advanced students were allowed
to take part, but klutes as young as nine or ten years
of age could be seen plummeting down the rock

faces practicing with their bows at times. They always had a parent or instructor with them, and were encouraged to stay at least thirty paces from the cliff when in free fall.

Students practicing without a parent or instructor were punished in demeaning ways, but not as seriously as they would be punished if they were actually caught in the Desowan or dropping in front of sivilin. The gusting winds along the cliff walls of the Sagitarian canyon had caused a few deaths and serious injuries over the years. Especially to young students.

Arak had failed to allow enough drift for the rapid downward trajectory of his body, and his arrow had been more than five feet below the sivilin's throat when it had thrown up its head. Not even close to the target. He realized that he was living one of the most intense experiences of his young life, and attributed nervousness combined with inexperience and sheer terror to the lousy shot. He streamlined his body as he'd been taught by Orem and his parents over the years, and soon he was falling headfirst at an incredible speed.

Arak spun himself until he could see the sivilin back up between the laced moccasins of his feet. It was about a hundred yards behind him in a full dive, but was falling much slower. The creature let out a shriek baring its teeth as if frustrated and Arak breathed a sigh of relief. They were safe for the moment. He began to survey his immediate surroundings, and saw that his friends were all close by. He could tell Enneka was laughing hysterically even though he couldn't hear him over the wind as they plunged headfirst with crossbows and wings carefully tucked against their bodies. He looked down and magnified his vision slightly trying to pick a nice spot in the thick forested valley below. Wind caused tears to cloud his vision for a moment but he squinted and was able to see clearings in the forest. A small tributary and trees in the secluded canyon directly below would protect them from the two hideous monsters that were descending upon them.

The klutes leveled off a few hundred feet above the ground then dropped into the small canyon. Soon they were safely hidden within the shade and boughs of two hundred foot tall pines, and giant deciduous trees that smothered and lined the banks of the medium sized brook with their long leafy branches.

Arak stood on the rough cracked surface of a huge branch and looked up through the green canopy. Shandra was in a big tree to his right, and Dulles had chosen a spot just across the creek for sanctuary. They couldn't see either of the sivilin, but the five of them remained quiet and motionless for more than fifteen minutes before Shandra finally broke the silence.

"They're gone." She said softly. Only Arak could hear her and he closed his eyes and sent an image of his arrow flying toward the sivilin. Shandra sent back a neural image that was almost identical. Her arrow had gone even lower than Arak's and had completely missed the giant flying lizard.

They waited a few more minutes before gliding to a clearing near the stream, then Dulles joined them. They were disappointed to find that his arrow had also been way off track, and had gone harmlessly below the creature.

Arak wasn't really very thirsty, but the crystal stream beckoned to him on the warm sunny day so he stooped down and took a drink before putting fresh water in his flask. Enneka and Rhee dropped from the canopy of branches across the stream as Dulles filled his flask. They had all been off their mark with their arrows. The five of them waited two hours to ensure safety before they lifted off and flew down the small canyon. They followed the creek staying near treetop level while watching for the sivilin. Dark clouds spanned more than half of the horizon to the northeast, and Enneka pointed.

"We'd better head for home." He said.

Arak didn't think the clouds looked that dangerous, and it was only about noon, but anything was possible with the unsettled weather and strong thermal convection over the delta during the hot humid months. Thunderstorm activity building up now would only strengthen as it continued moving to the southwest. They found a nice thermal a few minutes later and rose upward until they were just beneath a tight group of puffy white clouds.

They were above timberline when they began a slow lazy flight toward the distant gleaming summit of mount Sagitar. There were no sivilin to be seen, but another mass of convection was beginning to build up about an hour's glide to their south, and more dark clouds could be seen to the southeast.

"That doesn't look so good." Said Dulles. His left wing tip was about ten feet from Arak's right, and they were drifting with very little exertion with the eastward flow. The rising air between the two storms was pulling them upward and eastward to a height Arak had only experienced when rising above Mount Sagitar. Well over timberline and a half. They were probably in excess of sixteen thousand feet, but with hyperoxygenated blood they were in no danger.

"I don't think we can beat the storm." Said Enneka. "We might have to land and wait it out for awhile." He was right, and about half an hour later they decided to fold their wings and plummet between the converging storms. They spent four more hours in a large lean to at a well known campsite beside Moon Creek while lightning and thunder flashed and grumbled all around them. The storm was severe with intermittent rain and constant with lightning. After it finally abated they took flight in the cool fresh air.

The thunderstorm was moving slowly southeastward with a rare vortex flow so the small band of klutes hunted the nearby clearings along Moon Creek for about an hour before heading home. Small chura herds and lone mikta bucks were scarce or nonexistent, and they finally gave up. As the afternoon waned the storm actually seemed to intensify over the distant partially obscured mountains. Bursts of lightning tore open the sky sporadically as it seemed to linger over the narrow Sagitarian mountain range. It seemed to hover for a couple of hours, then the weak storm front finally lost most of its steam. The five young klutes were able to zig zag their way home between a couple of smaller thunderheads that were still building up over the delta.

Arak glanced around as he walked into the dining room of the academy, and was surprised that at least half of the students were still present. At least seventy young klutes from ages eight to seventeen were sitting on their benches at the short wooden tables scattered randomly around the cavern. He knew there had been some sort of meeting, or the place would be almost vacant by now. He spotted some of Rhee's friends sitting near the doorway to the kitchen. They waved to him, and Enneka followed him to their table.

Whit and her sister Kalli had both been served, and were almost finished eating, but there was room at the table for Arak, Enneka, Shandra and Rhee. Dulles had sent and received neural signals to and from his grandmother when they'd neared the colony, and he'd quickly disappeared into one of the upper caverns for roasted horat after they'd descended into the canyon.

Arak sat down and waited for the servers to come out of the kitchen with the evening's meal. They'd been tardy a few times, and Magahila, Orem, and Duroon knew the severe thunderstorm would cause some of the students to arrive late if they'd been on gathering or hunting tasks. No one would be punished or reprimanded. Arak nodded toward the wizened old imaging instructor when Orem entered the room.

Orem walked to the table and when Whit and Kalli stood to leave he sat down. Arak and Enneka conveyed him neural images of the two sivilin over Moon Creek. He was greying and his nose seemed a little too long for his face. His wings were scarred and sun bleached in places, but he was in excellent physical condition.

The instructor from the Glass Canyon asked them how their day went and his creased brow was wrinkled in thought while he closed his eyes to review the images Enneka started sending. He knew the youngsters were going to engage in skirmishes if the sivilin were over the western mountain front. He frowned for a moment, then laughed at the lousy shooting after he opened his eyes.

"Stay away from the sivilin." He said seriously. "And don't show Magahila or Duroon any images like this. From now on if you see any just try to avoid them." He laughed. "I don't know the circumstances involved with this attack but if you do have to shoot at one do it the same way, just aim higher. The elders are slowly changing, and I still don't consider myself one of them, but we actually talked about teaching students inverted trajectory archery at a younger age while at a meeting just a few days ago. I think I'm going to be put in charge of a new class just for this purpose. We want to start teaching some of the students in the fifth to seventh levels this summer." He scrutinized Arak and Enneka for a moment. "Day after tomorrow we'll go up the canyon to the cliffs and I'll let the five of you set up some targets if it's not too windy. Bring some stunners. Arak almost hit that damn thing in the neck."

Shilo was Orem's lifelong mate and when she suddenly made a rare appearance in the academy's dining room everyone stood and greeted her. She was the same age as Orem, just a little past middle aged, but not considered an elder yet. Her grey hair was long and straight, and she was very thin. She carried herself with a slightly regal manner and looked remarkably young for her age. She scrutinized everyone for a moment with intelligent blue eyes of the lightest shade, then she joined in conversation.

Pandemonium was reigning in Sagitar with scores of sivilin sightings and aerial combat was taking place daily. Cooking fires and warm meals were available until late at night in the academy, and usually all night in the main cavern below. Arak and Shandra ate dinner, drank warm teas and visited with younger students that had been at the meeting.

They found out that two more sivilin hunters had died over the Desowan in the past ten days. The news had arrived that morning when hunters had returned from a long excursion. According to some of the students, more of the giant flying predators were traveling in groups. Sometimes as many as five were being seen in one group, and they were landing and searching for hunters at times. This behavior was new, and very disturbing to all of the sivilin hunters. A meeting was to be held the following evening in the Sagitarian imaging sharing glacial cirque.

The next day was one of the most dreaded days in the academy for Arak. He absolutely despised the pottery class that was given by Magahila every nine or ten days. The five of them would join with two of the other younger classes, and work with reddish colored clay that had been brought from the eastern edge of the Desowan. It was almost the only time the five young klutes in Arak's class were kept in school for the whole day. Arak thought it was a waste of time when they could be practicing with their crossbows. Orem agreed with him, but Magahila and Duroon were from an old fashioned strict line of Sagitarian descendants, and they both insisted on sticking to the rules passed down by their forefathers.

There were eleven students from Sagitar in their graduating class for the present year, and most of the lessons had evolved into, or now pertained to simple hunting and gathering of food or crafting of other necessities for the Sagitarian colony while sorties of hunters flew out over the Desowan looking for sivilin. Arak could make arrowpoints very quickly from flint quarried in various locations throughout the delta, or obsidian brought from the glass canyons, and he'd even entirely constructed his last pine, sinew and rosin crossbow from scratch with very little help from Duroon or Orem. Duroon was considered the best of the best in Sagitar when it came to the crafting of pine hewn weapons used against the sivilin, and he was in complete charge of the archery crafting lessons for the entire colony.

Rhee smiled when Arak sat down next to her for breakfast prior to the pottery class. "I can't believe Orem is going to help us practice with our bows.

That was the most intense experience of my life yesterday."

Arak glanced behind them at a small younger group that had suddenly become too quiet as if eavesdropping.

He held a finger to his lips signaling her to speak more quietly or not at all, and she changed the subject.

"One of the hunters that got killed last week was a good friend of my father's." She said with a sad look. "I knew him. Some of the scouts came in yesterday and they have even seen some sivilin up near one of the low lying mountain ranges somewhere north of the Desowan. They are bringing bad news about the northern chura populations. Thousands of the animals used to run in herds up there in the patchy forested northlands. Now they are becoming very hard to find."

Arak was suddenly worried about his mother. It was becoming a commonplace occurrence to know someone or have a relative put out of action or killed by the invading scourge of giant flying reptiles.

"My mother went flying with Numak's wing today." Arak speared a chunk of rare reddish colored citrus fruit that had been delivered from the Mocktaw islands the week before. The fruit was as big as a flying moolara and had been sliced and placed on a shared plate in the center of the table.

Image sharing of the sivilin that had killed Rhee's mother were still imprinted in his mind; too graphic to share with any of the other younger students. Her body had literally been torn in half in mid-air by a pair of the giant winged lizards. Arak was the only friend that Rhee had confided the images with.

Shandra, Enneka, and Dulles soon arrived and the sun's rays slowly began creeping down the canyon rim south of Mount Sagitar turning the grey limestone and granite cliffs above the klute colony their usual various tinted orange hues beneath high cirrus clouds of an almost clear sky.

Magahila met them right after breakfast, and they followed her to the firing cavern where clay utensils were crafted. The morning went by slowly, and to the student's surprise Magahila left them by themselves for the whole afternoon. She said they could leave as soon as they'd each completed their projects, and had placed them in the oven for baking or firing.

Arak's was a simple jug with two handles, and he carefully painted the inside with a tough purple glaze pigment before attaching the top and bottom, and painting the outside. He was finished by early-afternoon, and waited a short time for Rhee, Dulles, and Enneka. Shandra said she had to do errands for her aunt, so when they were all done Orem and the other four flew up the canyon to the cliffs and began setting up targets. Arak loosened the leather straps on a pile of brightly colored but faded grass woven matts, and selected an orange and yellowish colored one before lifting off and picking a spot along the escarpment about a quarter of the way down.

Each of the other three selected a target to place below the summit of the highest vertical cliff wall. This would give them plenty of time to pull out of a dive even at terminal velocity. They placed the targets around and above the ledge that Arak had chosen, then they tied them in place with braided rawhide lines that were already dangling from cracks in the rock face. They clung to the wall as best they could and Arak laughed at Rhee who almost slipped while tying a loose bow around a faded reddish and purple colored matt with her teeth and one hand.

The four of them dropped from above the escarpment a couple dozen times before darkness, and as always Arak's arrows found the three foot matt almost every time while the rest of them struggled with an accuracy within a six or eight foot diameter. They were all using crude but perfectly straight stunner arrows that sometimes broke when they hit the rocky wall. Arak's training in the tricky gusts of the Glass Canyon colony with his father in his early years of flight were paying off. Orem was very pleased with them, especially Dulles who showed a huge improvement over his previous lesson, and of course Arak's almost professional marksmanship.

Miz would be in the Desowan for at least two or three days so Arak ate dinner with Shandra in the academy's dining room before going to the glacial cirque for the big gathering or meeting that had been planned two days earlier. She had bathed in the hot spring and looked pretty in winter white zinda fur slacks. Her jacket was made from a spotted yellow, brown and black prime taral skin and it accentuated her eyes making her even more stunning.

Orem, Maghila, Duroon, five of the other elders, and two supreme were present. Orem was supreme in the Glass Canyon colony and Savant in Sagitar. The meeting was brief and to the point. Image sharing portrayed two instances of sivilin stalking klutes that had landed in the Desowan wilderness. In one instance a Sagitarian klute had to dodge through trees while trying to elude a sivilin in the forested rocky terrain along the base of a long narrow mesa. The other attack also ended well with a klute from the Taro colony escaping a sivilin in a deciduous forested grove along one of the rivers.

Savant stood on the eight-foot rostrum stone with Orem and addressed a group of over four hundred after the image sharing. A discussion ensued, and it was decided that safe forested areas were to be mapped in better detail by scouts, and in sight whenever possible when dropping on sivilin over the Desowan. Another image was then shared by a scout from the Mocktaw islands, and it portrayed a group of seven sivilin soaring the volcanic islands nearest the shoreline south of Taro. Another pair had also been sighted over one of the human landwalker cities to the south. Klutes weren't safe anywhere it seemed; not even in the most distant islands where they enjoyed a popular but boring simple diet of fish, fruit, and crustaceans.

At the end of the meeting or image sharing a visiting female from Taro requested permission from Savant to project an unusual sighting. She was near the front so she was motioned to join the two supreme on the rostrum. She left her group and walked the twenty or so yards to the faint steps of the crude short carved stairway that wound from the front up around the back to the top of the imaging stone.

At first it was hard for Arak to tell what the projections were; it was simply a field of stars, but when the images became magnified through the visiting klute's eyes he could see movement in the skies. It appeared as if some of the brighter stars were drifting, moving, or perhaps being blocked by a shadow. After watching for a moment he was sure they were simply being blocked by a moving object. The visiting female's eyes were following the silhouette of a giant sivilin. A sivilin with a massive above average length wingspan. Stationary stars filled the backdrop as the dark shadow slowly drifted across the heavens. It wasn't the first image of this kind to be projected, and it was slightly disturbing. The sivilin were hunting or at least traveling at night sometimes. The winged lizards usually only flew during the daylight hours or at rare times when both moons were full. The creatures didn't have nocturnal eyesight. This one was flying under the light of only one crescent moon, and it was the red moon. Not nearly as bright as the larger silver moon.

After the meeting they drank tea beside cooking fires in the main cavern, then Arak went to his small cubicle or partially walled dwelling within his family's small cave. Sometimes Shandra would accompany him when his mother was gone, and they would stay in his room at his parent's tiny temporary domain.

Shandra was busy doing some kind of remodeling for the drafting of smoke in the kitchen of her aunt's upper cave. Her aunt Clove was in charge of several of the cooking fires and food preparations in the huge shared main cavern where visitors and sivilin hunters gathered for meals around the clock four, five, or even six times a day.

Arak started a quick fire in the tiny fireplace with coals he'd brought in his chura horn, then walked to the back of the cave and lit a couple of candles. He pulled back a tanned fur hanging and reached into the alcove. He got out his flint knapping tools and a few arrows he'd been working on. He noticed the old ceremonial projectile that had been given to him by his grandfather. The shaft was made from a rare piece of black greasewood found only in the Desowan wasteland, and it was ageless. Probably over five hundred years old. Maybe even seven or eight hundred. The sinew holding the obsidian points in place was mostly gone, and the feathered fletchings had turned to dust long ago, but the wood never rotted and both serrated razor sharp blades were still in their proper grooves in the thick shaft. His grandfather had found it laying beside the age darkened bones of a klute in an ancient grave. The bones had been exposed by a hungry taral in the back of a cave in the western valley above the Glass Canyon colony. It was different than anything he'd ever seen, and he'd been copying the quad bladed point with a few arrows of his own.

His grandfather had given him the double-bladed arrow when Arak was just learning how to ridge soar, and Arak had treasured it; always keeping it in a safe place. Sometimes he had strange dreams after handling the projectile, but his mother just attributed it to his imagination. He didn't really like the dreams. They were sivilin hunting dreams, and though he'd seen many neural images of actual sivilin encounters the dreams were different, and not connected to anything he'd witnessed at an image sharing. It was against Sagitarian policy for students to see or share graphic images, and some of the dreams were very disturbing, even horrifying with death and dismemberment. Sometimes at night he would be awakened by them.

He pulled a roll of twisted sinew and some rosin materials from the alcove, then began working on his third copy. He wrapped the sinew around the secondary blade which he'd inserted through an aperture behind the primary arrowhead. The hardest part was making the actual arrowhead and knife blade. The obsidian had to be serrated like a saw and razor sharp to mimic the artifact.

He used a thicker shaft similar to the ceremonial arrow, and when he was finished wrapping the point he dipped all three arrow tips into a small clay mug of boiling pine rosin that he'd mixed with chura fat. Arak then carefully wiped all of the blade edges before the mixture cooled, and placed the arrows on a shelf to dry. He put the ancient ceremonial projectile in his crossbow and made sure the secondary blade wasn't touching the bottom of the groove that he'd made slightly deeper to accommodate the thick shaft. It was the only modification he'd made to the bow for the quad bladed arrows.

He aimed his bow toward the wall and raised it to his shoulder. The weapon looked very formidable and sinister with the extra long blade sticking out. He wondered what sort of evil spirit it was supposed to ward off, and laughed out loud. He suddenly wondered about the strange dreams that seemed to be associated with the shaft, and wondered if a memory could somehow be surfacing from the wave rifts. A memory or vision from somewhere beyond the limits of time, or a klute's intelligence. Arak knew that nobody in his family really believed in spirits. It just looked like a better weapon to him, and he wanted a few of them in his quiver for his next encounter with a sivilin. Sometimes the elders talked about a time in the distant past before the glaciers had covered the delta. It was just a rumor or story, and there were no scrolls to corroborate it. A time long long ago when the klute race had almost met its demise, but not from a climactic change. A time when no place on the continent was safe from sivilin during daylight hours.

CHAPTER TWO

Cin stood on top of the icy summit and squinted in the bright sunlight while shading his eyes. Jagged rocky ridges reached skyward with their uneven profiles etching the horizons for as far as he could see in three directions. He'd been crossing the sea ice for almost two days, and was glad to have his feet on some solid ground again. He was cold, but not in any danger. It was early summer, and he would find warmth to the south in a few days. He ate a large chunk of salted chura and dropped from the icy promontory unfolding his wings. He felt alone suddenly and a forlorn sense of anxiety almost overwhelmed him, but he calmed himself and reverted to his belief in an existence of a level of intelligence that was above his understanding. He knew that something was always with him in his solo flights; connected somehow; watching perhaps.

The storm had blown in unexpectedly while he'd been soaring beyond the Serlian mountin range. He'd been flying above a low cloud ceiling when a gust front from the south unexpectedly began blowing him northward at an incredible speed. He'd thought about dropping through the clouds but had decided to ride it out for awhile.

He knew he was in trouble when he finally found broken cloud. There was nothing below him but ice floes and water, so he'd drifted onward. Cin knew he was in unexplored territory, and was slightly disconcerted and well as disoriented, but he'd been lost before.

He wasn't too worried, he knew he would be able to find enough food to make it back to familiar hunting grounds. One of the most practiced skills in a klute's upbringing was to survive and maintain composure when in dire situations. His father had sent him out over the ocean west of the Glass Canyon colony many times. He'd flown several hours beyond the coastal line of sight horizon, and had never had any problem making it back, but this was different. There weren't any stars or moons to watch and there were absolutely no images of any kind in the neural rifts. The sun never set here; it just circled three hundred sixty degrees and Cin had no way to tell time. The one advantage to flying above the north sea was ice. He could land and kill malara or perhaps other wildlife or forage for eggs if need be. There were probably predators on the ice but he'd never seen a white bront and knew they were very rare. He'd only seen two images of a northern or polar bront in his whole life at a sharing. His only worry was water. He didn't really like eating snow and without fire he would have no way to melt it.

He'd seen several groups of arctic sea malara, and knew he could kill one of the colorful sea creatures with his crossbow if need be. He'd never seen one before this, but quite a few images had been shared at some of the gatherings. Cin dropped to an altitude of about five hundred feet once when he sighted a group. He used slightly magnified vision to examine them closely, and found them almost comical looking as they gazed up at him. He wondered what they were thinking, and realized that they were afraid. Their spotted furry faces looked almost like someone had painted them on in various designs like snowflakes that were always slightly different in some way, yet the same. The three shades of camouflaged pale oranges, or light browns, greys, and whites were as random as the genetic pool was infinite. There were literally hundreds of them dotting the arctic landscape of sea ice and small desolate rocky islands. They would scurry into the watery holes and cracks between the ice whenever he drew near as if eluding perhaps a sivilin.

Not many klutes had flown across the strange arctic wilderness north of the Serlian mountains, and less had ventured out across the expanse of sea ice and small islands known as North Land's End. Probably because there was simply no reason to do so. Winter would obviously be the best time to watch the stars and Polaris in the constant darkness, but even this would be disconcerting without a way to tell time, and the sustained frigid climate during the dark months made life itself almost impossible even for a klute with hyperoxygenated blood. No one had ever returned from a long distance flight over the polar ice cap, and except for the Mocktaw Islands, flights far out to sea in any direction usually ended up the same way.

Those that had been north of the Serlian mountains had returned to the delta to share images, but mostly pictures of the icy ocean from the shoreline. There was really no point in trying to cross the sea and usually food or fire sources were a problem in the arctic. Of the very few that had ventured, no one had ever returned from a flight across the frozen northern expanse for some unknown reason.

Cin flew onward stopping several times when he became tired. He was able to hang his hammock out of the wind with long lines in crevasses between towering chunks of ice.

It took what he guessed was just over two days with no sight of land or any islands at all when he finally spotted another dark line on the horizon.

He vowed to be the first, to cross the strange jumbled mess of arctic sea ice and return, but not before resting a day or two and doing some hunting. Then he would extend his flight onward to the south for a few more days. The wind was still in his favor, and he should be able to keep transgressing a few hundred miles a day as he'd been doing.

He flew south for a few more hours and crossed another icy channel. As soon as Cin neared the next land mass he could see a shallow glacial fed stream running down a wide valley. He landed and filled his water flask. To his delight the stream was full of spawning fish, so he quickly searched the brushy area for a long shaft, and he made a double pronged spear. Cin was able to wade in amidst the fish with no problem and spear a couple. He was also able to find shelter along the waterway in a narrow ravine with some scrub brush where he could make fire, and a day later he was completely refreshed.

Flying in a selected direction in constant daylight was almost impossible so he simply drifted with the wind until he could tell when the sun was at a lower spot on the horizon showing him north. Luckily the weather was fairly clear with very few clouds of any kind. With no stars, or any way to tell time he would just have to use dead reckoning to guide him in what he hoped was a straight line and guess at the distances he was traveling. Dead reckoning had been tried while making flights across the sea to the south of the delta below a high cloud ceiling, but the Mocktaw Islands had four supreme, and all of them could project or receive images for six or seven hours glide time. Anyone making the journey could home in on a thread or neural singularity with another klute within five hours glide of any of the islands.

Keeping a timed instrument with fine sand steady enough while flying was very impractical. It was more practical to just fly at night in the warmer climate while watching the Polaris. Some very astute individuals could guess time and distance almost perfectly by watching the horizon in relevance to a few distinct stars or constellations. Destinations were just limited to approximately the six hours that it took to reach the northernmost of the Mocktaw islands, and no one had been lost at sea for years.

That evening as he drifted out of the mountains and onward with the ten to fifteen thousand foot southerly trade winds he wasn't surprised to find a tundra sort of like that which had been below him before the storm had blown him out over the icy sea or wide channel. The only difference was that there were hundreds of lakes of all shapes and sizes dotting the landscape, perhaps thousands. Cin was pretty sure he was exactly on the other side of the planet, but not positive, and he didn't think he was over a gigantic island but he wasn't sure.

The upper flow remained steady, as did the weather, and he drifted in a southerly direction for what he guessed was about two days and two nights as the sun circled him. He slept in his hammock for a few hours at two different rock outcroppings. Finally, the third day the sun began to get very low on the horizon behind him.

When darkness finally fell the next day, he watched colorful auroras flicker in reds, yellows, and greens at all points of the compass. He enjoyed the light show for an hour or so, then the destitute empty feeling of being completely alone became almost overpowering. Cin had been in the same forlorn solitary situation for long stretches of time before, and shrugged off his emotions. He looked down at the desolate denuded landscape from about half timberline or five thousand feet. It seemed as if the sun rose almost as soon as it set, and he hoped that if there was a god, or higher power of some kind that it was watching him right now. He'd been lost before, and the uncanny feeling was familiar, but just as disconcerting as it had been the first time when he was young and just learning to fly beyond the line of sight horizon at night.

Cin followed the friendly star formations with which he was familiar. He could see the four stars in a long arc that defined the back of the zinda. Three more stars arced slightly upward to the left of the zinda's back defining the tail and tip that pointed exactly toward the northern Polaris a short distance directly above, while three slightly brighter stars at the opposite end defined the head and ears of the constellation. He quelled an innate sense or instinct as he flew south away from his home and his family on the delta knowing he should be flying toward it from the opposite side of the narrow arctic sea or channel.

He decided to look for a place to land. Cin began looking for a rock outcropping or grove of brush where he could get out of the wind and build a fire to raise his core temperature. He saw a group of high rocky bluffs stretching across the lake filled landscape toward the southwestern horizon about an hour later, and banked for a look. There was a grassy sheltered basin in the center of the highest knoll, so he landed on the lee side near a khiska thicket and dozed beside a fire for about six hours.

The country was partially covered with snow from springtime storms, but summer had arrived, and there were green spots sprouting and spreading quickly as grass that had been frozen in the long nights of the arctic winter months began to breathe new life from the sun. There was also animal life here that had already migrated north, and after dark he could see a few chura of a larger northern species grazing between the protective boulders and crevasses of the dozens of rocky promontories that dotted the permafrost below him.

Cin flew onward, watching the stars of the brief night sky carefully for direction. Two days later he was over lush green plain like that south of the Serlian mountains only with more lakes. It had been receiving sunlight for almost a month and in some places grass was knee deep. There were stubby stunted pine groves amongst the hills now and rocky eroded crevasses, but the trees were only about a third as tall as the pines of the delta, and some on the exposed northern slopes only grew branches on one side due to the cold wind. The only animal life he saw were a few sivilin grazing far below on his fifth day south. Any sivilin sighting always meant that there were more in the area, and he kept a sharp lookout in the airspace surrounding him using magnified vision at times for the next couple of days.

A week after crossing the polar sea he found another reason why there was perhaps an absence of herbivores on the bare exposed northern tundra. Cin was about to turn back toward the north and head home. He was fighting a disgustingly strong headwind after skimming a high rocky reef of sawtooth mountains at about half timberline when he was viciously attacked from the air, but not by a sivilin.

The flying lizards were almost as big in body size as a zinda, but not quite. They had wide leather wings that were attached to their sides, and extended from a flexible multiple jointed hollow bone sort of like a klute, but they were also attached to half of their front legs. The appearance was almost that of a large flying kite in a way, but they had a sleek controllable wing span connected to the sixth appendage of about fifteen feet. He was sure they weren't very aerobatic, but they had a long, webbed tipped tail to help guide them, and he was a little bit surprised at their dexterity. They also had the immediate advantage of altitude.

The gliding or flying pack descended from somewhere above him in the rocky serrated cliffs like they hadn't eaten for days, and they were probably confident that they could acquire Cin as an easy meal or at least kill him to protect their territory. They'd never encountered a klute, especially a klute from the tricky gusts of the Glass canyons. Luckily there weren't very many.

Cin rolled and dodged the first one while untying his crossbow from the sling that kept it in its resting place at his side. Two more of the flying predators were closing in at an alarming rate as he tucked his wings for a dive that would take him to terminal velocity in a matter of seconds. One of them went for his leg as it dropped past, but Cin was able to whack it with the end of his bow and keep it away from him. He noticed that it had long retractable claws like a huge cat or zinda, and it knew how to use them. The flying predator almost tore the bow out of his grasp.

The second one collided with him and locked onto his shoulder with its teeth, but luckily the straps from his backpack and his tanned leather jacket kept them from sinking very deep. Cin kept the clawing feet and legs away from him by rolling to the side, and he pulled one of his obsidian knives from the sheath on his belt. He ran it to the hilt in the side of the reptile while the third one closed in again. The one that he'd stabbed shrieked loudly and when it let go of his shoulder he stabbed it deeply in the throat almost severing its windpipe. Cin stabbed it again and used the stock of his crossbow as a lance to keep the other two away from him as they all fell together. His crossbow had dozens of teeth and claw marks on it before he reached a speed that kept him a safe distance from the creatures. He cocked it and shot one, then the other with precision accuracy. Wind resistance was uncompromised by the direction between himself and the predators directly above.

The battle had seemed to last a long time, but it was actually over in a matter of seconds, and Cin pulled out of his dive less than a thousand feet above a hilly green forest that was splotched with patchy clearings and meadows. He watched the attacking bodies plummet to their resting places, and then followed. He found one of the crossbow bolts and was happy to find it completely undamaged with the obsidian point deeply embedded in a rib inside of the lizard. The other projectile had deflected off of bone and had passed through the body of its target.

Cin began searching for a secluded spot for himself. His shoulder was sore, and he had some scratches and cuts on his arms and one of his legs. One that might cause problems. He needed to cleanse the wounds and scrub them with disinfecting healing powders from Sagitar that Miz had placed in his knapsack. He realized that the lizards hadn't been very acrobatic compared to a klute, more comparable to large sivilin. Cin had found them almost clumsy, and he realized that he would have a very unusual memory to share at the next gathering in the cathedral at Sagitar. There were small flying lizards in the Desowan wasteland; usually no more than a couple feet long, and they were harmless and very skittish. His clothes would need some mending, but that project would have to wait.

Another long narrow rocky projection rose from the hills to the south and it almost spanned the horizon, so he headed for the intermittent limestone and granite cliffs hopeful that he might find a shelter or a cave of some kind without encountering more dangerous predators in the air. He carefully scanned the area with enhanced vision before heading for a dark shaded opening that caught his attention. About five minutes later he banked sharply to the right and descended. Gnarly pines and brush covered the nearby area, and firewood was plentiful. He soon had a fire inside of the rock shelter that had been used by wolflike madas, and even some kind of cloven hooved animals in the past. The wolf scat was the most plentiful.

After he tied long branches together at the top, and jammed the other end of a long pole in a cleft in the cliff wall, he was able to sleep in his lightweight hammock. The night only lasted about four hours here, but it was obvious he'd come quite a distance south since crossing the icy sea.

His shoulder was fine, and the next day he killed wild game along the base of the cliff wall. The tiny wooly tusked quadrupeds were practically invisible against the light grey limestone background, and he guessed that camouflage was probably their best means of defense against, flying lizards, sivilin, or whatever landwalking predators were prowling the countryside. Cin was lucky enough to spot them as they crossed a grassy area, and he swooped for a kill shot. The rest of the herd ran and climbed into the rocks almost instantly disappearing into the maze of shadowy crevasses and cracks within the small canyons of the escarpment. He'd never seen animals of this species anywhere in his life. Not even beyond the Desowan wilderness, and the flying lizards had also been a terrifying new experience.

A warm southern wind blew with a fury the next day, so he just stayed in the shelter and rested while preserving or smoking the backstraps and hind quarters of the herbivore. The lizard attack had enticed him to explore a little farther to the south. There were no scroll recordings of such an animal or predator.

Cin continued southward for a few more days after the attack, and he was able to find thermals and soar to heights that kept him safe in a flow that had switched and was coming out of the northwest at about twice glide speed. He spotted five of the smaller flying lizards with his magnified vision the day after leaving his mountain shelter, and gave them a wide berth. That evening he spotted two sivilin far below, and took advantage of a fast shifting northeastward flow before using his hammock in the pines of a tiny white water canyon.

He almost seemed to be in a vortex or center of a dangerous cold front that was descending from the north the next day, and he had to spend another night out of the wind in a huge open mouthed cave or shelter beneath a giant bluff. Limestone and granite rims rose along a wide stream here and Cin started a fire. He ate the last of the rations from his pack as the storm unleashed lightning that flickered and danced above the peaks. Rain and hail accompanied the thunder and lightning for a couple of hours along the edge of the front, and he knew some of the electrical strikes were very close.

He sat beside his fire and watched sheets of rain and hail pelt the swaying evergreens outside of the cave entrance until the storm finally abated. His hammock was useless so he simply slept while leaning against the wall; wings folded around him for warmth.

The next morning he rose with the sun, and stretched, while unfurling his wings. He turned around and noticed some darker areas on the cracked rock wall. At first they just looked like naturally occurring pigment within the stone; then suddenly one caught his complete attention. It was a remarkable representation of a chura. The horns and all four feet; even the hooves had obviously been drawn on the cave wall with charcoal or some sort of black pigment by a previous visitor. Perhaps a landwalker. He strolled slowly around the huge cavern and found a dozen more drawings or pictographs. Most of them appeared to be ancient with lichens and moss growing on them, but some looked like they could possibly be more recent.

The hills rose higher and higher the next day causing him to soar to an altitude well above timberline to remain five or six thousand feet above ground level. A ceiling of spotty cloud at about a thousand feet, and a gradual absence of vegetation began to worry Cin, but he continued on south until he saw another mountain range sticking up above the broken cloud ceiling.

The erosion of the canyons and deep rocky valleys below him resembled a landscape somewhat like that of the most rugged in the Desowan wilderness, but here there was almost complete absence of vegetation and the wind was incessant at lower elevations. Some of the canyons seemed to drop away into dark grey rocky crevasses of shadowy oblivion they were so deep. Ahead were the mountains that had been carved, and were still surrounded by the glaciers that fed the streams that had helped cut the canyons.

The highest peaks in front of him rose to at least timberline and a half or above. Cin wondered if they were even higher than Mount Sagitar itself. There were several small herds of the wooly tusked animals grazing along the high benches and grassy ledges, and as always they quickly disappeared into pine chocked cracks, crevasses, canyons, and even small caves when they saw him. He finally got one with his bow but it was difficult cutting the meat from the carcass on the thin ledge where it fell. The cold wind at elevation made it even more so. Luckily for him there were no flying lizards of any kind around.

He was glad to see one of the moons rise well before midnight, and as he drifted southward he was able to get a sense of direction without checking for the Zinda constellation and Polaris. He soared through a pass with serrated terraced granite on both sides as the bright three quarter moon loomed on the distant western horizon off to his right. It looked much larger than normal because of the lens effect of the planet's atmosphere. The red moon still hadn't risen, but it would by midnight, and Cin felt confident as he rode a cold katabatic flow in a crystal, clear sky away from the mountain range. He soared above foothills and glacial moraine that was divided by canyons and valleys cut by the erosion from past millions of years.

Cin had been searching for something for six years while sivilin hunting and scouting. Something that seemed to be non-existent anywhere within klute hunting grounds or even in the Desowan. He'd seen the liquid six or seven years before, and it had amazed him beyond belief. The strange viscous fluid had given off a peculiar odor that could almost be mistaken for that of a sulfurous hot spring. He'd watched the landwalkers use it to make light in their cities. It was different than tos oil or other animal fats, or even plant or palm oils including any mixture. The liquid burned with an explosive intensity when enough of it was ignited at the same time.

Cin knew it came from somewhere beneath the ground, and he'd looked for it to no avail around coal seams in the Desowan. The landwalkers brought small quantities from a spring near a giant walled crater near one of their cities, but the seeping well produced only a miniscule amount each week, and sometimes nothing. He'd heard an ancestral rumor of a fluid that seeped from the black coal sands somewhere in a chasm in the northern wilderness. The fluid burned on its own like the sap from a desert pine, but there were no images to prove it, and searching for it seemed to be futile. Everyone had been alerted to look for the explosive fluid for possible uses as a weapon against sivilin, but so far nothing much had been found. Just some thick tarry sands that were almost impossible to ignite.

Scattered pines began growing in groves as he soared southward in the darkness. Cin soared thermals or lift from the convection of a wave or cold front. He could see long timbered valleys ahead and below with rugged forested hilly terrain to each side of a long wide slow moving stream that stretched to the southeastern horizon. Another huge mountain range swathed in snow and glacial icefields rose on the southern end of the immense valley.

Cin landed in the forest alongside the river after scouring the area for predators, then he removed his pack. He drank from the stream and started a little fire beneath a giant pine where the flames wouldn't be noticed. He cooked fresh meat using the back-straps of the wooly animal and strung his hammock high in the tree. A pair of large feathered mawls flew over screeching from time to time, and he could hear several other types of smaller wildfowl either on the ground or hopping and flying around in the higher branches of the nearby trees.

When Cin unrolled his hammock and secured it to the limb which he was standing on he couldn't help noticing the huge pine cones drooping from the branches. The moonlight was bright with help from both moons, and he plucked a nearby one by twisting it with some difficulty. He carefully pried the seed pods apart exposing a nut as big as a small sized arrowhead. A tiny furry flying moolara chat-tered at him from a branch about twenty feet above almost as if Cin were robbing its pantry. He glanced upward, and the grey and black striped animal sud-denly leapt and glided off to another tree with small leather like wings that unfolded with its legs. He'd eaten pine nuts from several smaller cones, on the delta or in the Desowan wilderness, and had never experienced any ill effects. The nuts were delicious, and he pulled the pods apart until he'd robbed the two foot cone of ten large mature seeds. Cin ate a few of them and set the rest near his hammock. He'd experienced stomach aches from divulging in strange foods, usually brought from the Mocktaw Islands, and he had learned to be careful.

The next morning he dropped from the huge evergreen and stretched his wings wide for an easy bank that took him out over a good sized grassy clearing with little effort. There were miktas near the edge and they quickly disappeared into the foliage toward the river. The animals were about the same size as the deltan miktas, but the snow white hair on their underbellies and the insides of their legs slightly differentiated the two species. Cin left them where they were and flew up out of the forest.

The lush green timber stretched for as far as he could see with steep rocky cliffs and granite outcroppings poking their crumbling faces and cracked pointy peaks out of the forest on each side of the turquoise tinted stream. The terrain ahead was rising to the snowpack and glaciers of the mountain range he'd seen in the moonlight the night before.

Cin circled and carefully made a mental image of the clearing and his camping place in accordance with a high cliff wall and a curve to the east by the river. He had a photographic memory as did almost all klutes, and would be able to retrace his flight exactly, and find his belongings after exploring the nearby intriguing countryside. He realized that he was probably at a latitude about equal with that of the Glass Canyon or Sagitarian colony, and the surrounding landscape was beautiful, perhaps even more so than that of the klute's forested treasured hunting grounds north of the Wind River or Moon Creek outposts. There was a pristine sense of cleanliness in the fresh air above the high valley, and Cin noticed that timberline was low on the intense terrain of the icy granite mountains ahead. He was flying at an altitude near timberline and he was only about three thousand feet above the trees and glacial fed stream.

Thermals were weak, and he was forced to use his wings from time to time to maintain his present elevation in the thin air. He scoured the sky as always for dangerous predators, and was glad to find it empty. A notch in the granite loomed ahead at about timberline and a quarter, and he was soon drifting up through a narrow chasm toward the opening with the wind behind him. The farther up the canyon he rose the faster the wind pushed him with a venturi effect produced by the narrowing of the canyon. He shot through the vee shaped pass at a nice speed using his wings to keep him well above the sharp rocky summit, and was surprised to see a panorama dotted with large and small lakes stretching to the distant eastern horizon. The river appeared to wind around through a canyon to the west and drain into one of them.

Cin took advantage of the thermals and gusts along the craggy peaks and soon soared to an altitude requiring stored hyperoxygenated blood from his spleen. He banked for a slight descent above the rocky glacial canyon to the west that the river plunged through. The terraced rugged canyon caused mist to rise from falls along the cascading stream as it cut its way toward the huge eastern lake. Some of the vertical drops were many hundreds of feet. He suddenly felt a vague tiny spiking or tingling in the back of his head and was startled. He closed his eyes briefly and tried to get a better sense of direction; there had definitely been a presence or singularity in the neural rifts.

He soared the winds rising along the highest nearby mountain peaks and searched the wave rifts for almost an hour to no avail. The singularity or presence remained silent. Cin decided to wait where he was for a day or two and see if he could discover the source of the weak neural link, and he began searching the wide pine valley for miktas. He didn't care much for the greasy fat streaked meat of the wooly animals.

He was lucky and killed a buck about an hour later just upstream from his camping spot. The mikta buck had the biggest and most unusual antlers he'd ever seen on an animal of comparable size. Each of the main branches of the animal's armament produced four or five long sharp points almost like the horns of a shadowbeast, and smaller points protruded from them in various random places. Cin wished he were nearer home, as the animal's rack would make an excellent and very unusual ornamental clothing hanger, or perhaps just a rustic conversation piece in one of the cooking caverns of Sagitar. The miktas of the delta and Desowan had smaller simple spiked or forked antlers without hardly any other pointed projections.

He butchered the animal then carefully used the hide to wrap and place the choicest cuts in his backpack. He hadn't seen a zinda since leaving the delta, but the semi-nocturnal cats were around He could hear them fighting over the rest of the carcass a few hours after the kill. Cin had already cooked, and was resting in his hammock when the commotion awakened him. He quickly rolled from his hammock unfolding his wings as he dropped from the branches. He decided to have a look at them.

The bright moon was overhead, and the zindas were soon visible on the forest floor in the clearing where he'd left the mikta carcass. It was a rare sight. On the delta the cats would usually remain hidden in the forest until the bright moon was almost below the horizon. There were three of them. Two of them were taking turns ripping pieces from the carcass then retreating a short distance while the larger one indulged itself at leisure. They were dark colored, almost black with light brown stripes. They appeared just about identical in size to the zindas of the delta, but he couldn't be sure. Cin watched them for a few minutes and realized that they were aware of his presence, but unconcerned. Except for the klutes or human landwalkers, the Zinda was an unchallenged apex predator. It appeared that this was the case here also, but these zindas seemed to be completely unafraid, almost as if there were no such thing as a klute, or a landwalker.

Cin rose high above the moonlit landscape for a short time and scanned the wave rifts again. He was surprised to feel another slight stirring for a few seconds, but there was nothing he could link to, just some static that quickly faded away. Something kept attracting his attention to the west, but it wasn't any kind of neural signal, it was simply a faint orange glow or brighter area along the distant horizon. the red moon was still an hour below the horizon so he didn't know what was causing the glow. He guessed fire.

He returned to his hammock and retired for the evening. His remarkable spleen allowed him to sleep fairly comfortably with almost no coverings even if the temperature dropped to near freezing.

CHAPTER THREE

Arak stood on the ledge and enjoyed the warming rays of the early morning sunrise. The elders had changed, and they'd been letting the older students practice more along the Thunder cliffs as the summer wore on. He pulled the awning aside and tied it off. He was looking forward to a day of target practice along the high cliffs and he quickly slung his pack. He wore lightweight tanned leather clothing fashioned for summer, and lightweight moccasins.

The young klute unfolded his wings, and dropped from the small cavern that was set into the east side of the curved cliff wall of the Sagitarian colony. He drifted down to the wide wooden walkway along the front of the academy's kitchen and immediately saw Rhee and Shandra sitting at a table close to the door waiting for their breakfast. They were both also clad in tight fitting dark leather, and Shandra looked especially attractive wearing a revealing moolarine fur. A dozen or more shoulder length braids hung loosely circumventing her face, and were all tied at the ends with colored bands. Rhee was probably the least attractive of the two because of her chubby figure and face. Her hair was tied back and braided into two big knots for more practical reasons.

"Where are Dulles and Enneka?" he asked as he looked around the room. One of the younger students sitting close behind at another table moved his chair so Arak had room to pull a seat up between Shandra and Rhee.

"They might start letting us shoot along the Thunder rims tomorrow." The youngster held up his small crossbow and showed Arak. Arak didn't know half of the young student's names at the table, and he nodded. His bow lay on his pack by the door and it had almost twice the tension and pull.

Arak smiled and sat down. "Orem told us yesterday. He must have talked with the elders last night."

"It's about time." Said Shandra. "We should be able to defend ourselves from sivilin as soon as we start hunting."

"I agree." Rhee frowned. "But it does kind of seem like a waste of time with the small weapons."

Shandra sipped her tea and put the mug down. "My father says we need to find out where they're coming from and do something about it at the source. I like defending myself by staying away from them like we did the other day, but I also like living in Sagitar."

Arak leaned forward and plucked a couple of thin sausages from a platter that had just been placed on the table. "Scouts are flying all over looking for lairs, or some kind of colossal hatching grounds. Orem and Duroon think the sivilin are just reproducing in the eastern Desowan at an accelerated rate for some reason. Orem says the warmer climate is causing it."

"Enneka and Dulles are late as usual." Shandra sipped her tea again and glanced out at the distant cliff wall. The main cavern of the colony was just visible above the boardwalk. It was straight across the small valley and the small turquoise glacial tributary that flowed into the Sagitarian river. It was called Froze to Death creek. A sortie of sivilin hunters was just returning from a night's journey somewhere over the Desowan. Darkness was the only time they were completely safe from the sivilin at low altitudes, but on westward flights it was usually easy to make headway at a high altitude due to the tradewinds.

"I wonder which group that is?" Rhee was also watching the hunting party as they glided down onto the boardwalk above the hot spring at the mouth of the giant cave. "I counted eight."

"Not Numack's wing." Said Arak. "My mom went with them yesterday morning. Six of them I think."

Enneka and Dulles dropped down from their higher caverns within the next half hour, and they all ate a light breakfast before acquiring stunner crossbow bolts from the academy's nearly depleted arsenal. The weapons were all kept in a nearby vacant cavern just up the walkway from the kitchen. The main cave was almost vacant, but Duroon was getting ready to start teaching a group of the younger students some basic imaging lessons and they were beginning to arrive.

There were plenty of the blunt thick shafted stunners to go around, but some were missing a few feathers from the frequent use. Arak placed five in his quiver. The rest of them took a few more than Arak, and Dulles, and Rhee completely emptied her quiver and filled it with the thick blunt stone tipped target arrows.

Dulles put seven arrows in his quiver and looked at Shandra sheepishly. "I couldn't hit the matt at all yesterday."

Shandra laughed and smiled. "I broke a few tips off the last time I practiced up there too, and I lost one but the wind was blowing."

She'd missed the target practice the day before, and was carefully going through the dusty stack in a hollowed out anteroom of the back wall looking for the straightest of the crude blunt arrows. She was becoming a deadly shot.

She'd noticed more than a hint of frustration when Dulles had dumped all of his hunting bolts out on the floor. Sivilin hunting was altogether different than killing wild game for food.

Magahila had a wrapped lunch for each them made of chura jerky and of course lystroot, and she said that her and Orem would meet them at the Thunder cliffs an hour later. She told them to go ahead and set up their targets, so they stocked their packs quickly, and dropped out of the academy one at a time unfurling their wings at the entrance. The thermals were beginning to stir, and Shandra was very lucky. She seemed to have an extraordinary ability to sense when she was rising ever so slightly, and she circled in a fifty, yard wide column. Arak followed her and they rode the rising air upward until it became stagnant at about timberline. The thermal was short lived, but it had given them a huge altitude gain while the rest of the group struggled with simple ridge lift along the mountain front in the cooler morning air.

Mount Sagitar loomed off to the right and the students soared rising air along the near vertical slopes using their wings to push slowly northward.

Arak could see the rest of the group below at about seventy five hundred feet. They'd split up searching for thermals, and he was glad to see two of them finally begin to circle in a warmer column. Shandra pulled up alongside and they pushed against a slight northwest flow toward the high cliffs that lay less than fifteen minute's glide ahead.

The high point of Mount Sagitar slowly dropped behind, and they could see the Desowan wasteland and sandhills off to the east. They soared along the summit of the plateau between Mount Sagitar and Thunder mountain. The latter was only about five hundred feet shy of Mount Sagitar's highest point. The barren rocky pass was a thousand feet below that. It was the most popular route into and out of the Desowan by sivilin hunters.

Arak saw them first. The two sivilin were just coming around the northwestern side of Thunder mountain, and they were dropping rapidly in a shallow dive along the mountain ridge.

"Sivilin." He pointed and Shandra saw them immediately. The two of them were way higher than the sivilin at an altitude almost even with the top of Mount Sagitar, and they were still above the pass.

"Are they going after the others?" She asked.

Arak was in a quandary and couldn't see any of their friends below. He didn't hesitate. He tried to contact Enneka through the wave rifts but was unsuccessful.

"Stay close to me." He folded his wings into a controlled swept position. Arak pulled into a dive in a trajectory that would almost intersect that of the giant flying reptiles. He cocked his crossbow then reached into his quiver and pulled an arrow, but saw that it was a thick shafted target stunner. He simply dropped it. The next one he pulled out was one of the new double bladed copies of the ceremonial arrow. He angled it into the groove through the curved aperture helix at the end of his bow, and notched it securely. The helix and the notch at the base of the arrow would hold the projectile in place in wind resistance during most diving circumstances.

Arak scanned the area as he fell, and finally saw two of the others. They were already aware of the sivilin, and were dropping safely toward the forest below. He looked back at Shandra who had a wing tip only five feet to the right of his, and slightly behind, then corrected his dive slightly. She followed suit, and they fell toward the sivilin at about half terminal velocity.

Arak thought about breaking off the attack, but realized that he and Shandra were in a perfect position. They should be able to fire arrows and make it to safety with no problem.

The giant winged lizards were still at about three quarters timberline so he stayed his course. He was glad that Shandra had been able to load and cock her crossbow while in flight. They both shot past the left hand sivilin at about a quarter terminal velocity. The thing was surprised and raised its head quickly, but Arak was ready for the motion this time.

He pointed and aimed his crossbow judging for wind resistance and his speed in correlation with that of the target as he plunged past. When the sivilin lifted its head Arak had raised his aim an extra four feet and he'd already pulled the trigger. Shandra was right beside him and he saw her arrow streak forth as they tucked wings and weapons for a maximum dive that would take them to terminal velocity in a few seconds.

Arak failed to see where Shandra's arrow had gone, but was very pleased with his shot. His crossbow bolt had struck the sivilin in the throat right below its jaw, and had almost penetrated the entire length of the shaft. He glanced to the side and was pleased to see her looking back toward the flying monster with a smile on her face. She'd been very brave to load and fire her crossbow, but Arak had expected her to try a shot. They were outdistancing the sivilin, and the tangled forest in the rugged canyon below Thunder mountain would keep them safe indefinitely.

Both of the creatures were following them, but the one with the arrow in its throat was shrieking and clawing at its throat. The motion was slowing its fall. The two klutes were at least a half mile ahead of the attacking monsters when they pulled out of their dive near the large tributary of the Sagitarian river. The water in Thunder creek was a light turquoise from the sediment of the mountain glaciers wherever whitewater wasn't cascading over boulders. Arak leveled out about fifty feet above the fast moving medium sized stream with Shandra mere feet to his right. He turned his head and glanced back at the sivilin, but could only see one of them before selecting a nice opening beneath the forest canopy.

The two klutes disappeared into the trees beneath high leafy branches and pine boughs that would hide and protect them. Only one of the giant reptiles had followed them close to the ground, and Arak could see the shadowy outline of the thing as it glided overhead just a few hundred feet above. He could see no sign of the one he'd shot, and guessed it had broken off the attack.

"I missed completely." Shandra turned her head and looked at Arak. She grinned; her light green eyes were dilated with excitement and seemed almost translucent when a ray of sunlight crossed her face. She was breathing rapidly, and her voice was a little higher pitched than normal. "But I tried."

They'd both chosen the same ancient leafy tree as their refuge, and Arak stood on a wide branch about five feet from her. He walked down the limb bracing himself with another big side branch that was even with his head. He had to push leaves and small branches out of the way in a few places.

She followed him down through the smaller branches that sprouted upward, and met him in the fork of the five foot diameter tree trunk. They watched and listened for a few minutes, but the sivilin didn't return. It had flown off somewhere perhaps looking for its wounded mate or sibling.

"I got it right below the jaw." Arak looked at her and sent an image of his arrow buried to the feathers in the soft skin of the monster's upper throat.

Shandra had closed her eyes, and she exclaimed in awe when she perceived the neural signal.

"My arrow went low." She said. She sent back the images of her unsuccessful attempt, and Arak laughed.

"You almost hit it between the legs. I just sort of guessed about how the others raised their heads when I aimed, and my shot was lucky."

He suddenly felt a familiar tingling sensation in the back of his head, and closed his eyes. It was Enneka and Rhee both at the same time. He had trouble distinguishing between the neural signals for a few seconds before he made a link with Enneka's stream of images. He could sense Shandra as she also perceived the neural link, then he was completely shocked at the pictures that began to take form. The sivilin that Arak had shot had broken off the attack, and had turned toward the north slope of Thunder mountain while shaking and throwing its head violently.

"You got it!" Shandra looked at him wide eyed. "You turned it back with one arrow!"

Arak had also opened his eyes, and he looked at her. "I used a copy of my quad bladed ceremonial arrow. It has a wider arrowhead and an extra knife blade that I made with obsidian from the Glass Canyon."

Arak had just performed a task that would make him the envy of the Sagitarian colony for a few days if they shared images of the deed. He'd fired the perfect shot. Quite a few crossbow bolts would probably fly toward sivilin before another single bow shot was made that achieved such drastic and immediate results.

"I've seen the one in your room. I've never seen another arrow like it. I wonder whose idea it was to put double bladed serrated points on the shafts?" Shandra removed her knapsack, and sat down on the branch using the tree trunk and pack as a backrest.

"We'll never know." He answered. "But I'm going to make some more."

Songbirds were singing in the green canopy above them and a grey moolara scolded them from a nearby tree. It promised to be another hot summer day.

Arak also removed his pack, and they rested and watched the sky. There was no sign of the second sivilin.

"Someone in the Glass Canyon started making them generations before my grandfather was born." He looked in his quiver. "My father used some of the quad blades, but said they were mostly ceremonial weapons that would be placed beside someone who had passed away to ensure safety on the journey to the spirit world. Orem's father said that perhaps the double bladed projectiles had been used in a more dangerous time, perhaps to ward off sivilin or some other enemy. Maybe even another unfriendly klute race. Everyone I showed it to said it was a waste of time because they always broke off where the knife blade weakens he shaft. My father said the same thing, but he used some on chura and maybe a zinda. He said they didn't go between the ribs as well so he didn't bother making any more."

He pulled one from his quiver and handed it to her. The shaft was much thicker than hers with a circumference almost as big around as two of his fingers. A second razor sharp serrated obsidian point or blade had been inserted through a long thin aperture below the foremost arrowhead. The second blade had a simple square tip like the base where it was inserted inside the shaft, and it was tied in place with sinew and rosin on both ends. Razor sharp serrated glass shards stuck out more than an inch and a half on each side and hooked back behind the foremost point that was about two and a half inches wide. The quad tipped missile was tipped with obsidian points almost the size of a spearhead; much wider than Arak's other arrowheads.

"I had to cut a deeper groove in the end of my bow stock for the thicker shaft, but it shoots very well." He showed her the crossbow. I was thinking about making longer shafts, but I just copied the old ceremonial arrow that my grandfather gave me. I made three of them as identical as I could. The deeper groove in the bow actually helps hold the arrows in place when falling."

She'd seen them before, and nodded. "It's a very good idea. If we go over the Desowan someday I want you to make me a couple, or show me how you cut the hole through the shaft."

"That's the hard part." He answered. "I used an ivory awl to get a groove started; then a thin saw. The first couple of saws I made broke, but I finally switched to flint instead of obsidian and got a curved one that works pretty well."

They received another neural link from Rhee, and could see that they would have to remain where they were for awhile. The second sivilin was still circling the nearby area about a thousand feet above the ground.

The conversation with Shadra gave Arak an idea that would kill some time. He looked through his pack and pulled out a thin braided line that had been carefully tanned and coated with chura oil. One end was tied to a fair sized barbed hook made with ivory of a tusked sea malara from the coast north of the Glass canyon. The two of them glided down to the grassy pine needle carpeted floor and began searching for familiar insects that could be used as fish bait. Shandra caught one first and she brought him a big fat long legged green moth that had been clinging to a nearby leaf.

They walked to the river's edge while carefully scanning the sky, and selected a shaded rocky peninsula that jutted out into the main stream causing a deep backwater pool. A giant leafy tree that was probably starting to grow when Arak's great grandfather was a child offered shelter. It was close to the edge of the small river, and Arak threw the line into the deep whirlpool beneath the sanctuary of a friendly branch above them They didn't have to use quartz with firestone to spark the fire. Shandra produced coals from a chura horn she'd brought along, and she had a fire going as soon as Arak pulled a two foot fish from the pool. She used spices from a leather pouch and with forked sticks they soon had the fillets speared and wrapped on a rotisserie.

"Why did you bring fire?" Asked Arak.

"I don't know." She answered. "I guess I thought we might make one to heat sausages while we were practicing along the cliff."

"Magahila would be disappointed." Said Arak.

"What?" She looked at him as she sprinkled spice on the fillets."Why?"

"The lunch she wrapped for us is a special one today." He laughed. "I looked in mine and she even put a chunk of hardened niloberry syrup in there. She wouldn't want us wasting our time fishing."

Shandra walked to where her pack lay and she untied the back flap. "You know, she always seems worried about us when we go hunting, and even more so when we do target practice along the Thunder cliffs. She's very strict, but I think she enjoys shooting the targets while falling as much as we do."

She unrolled the thin tanned leather wrapping and laughed. "She meant to surprise us."

The rest of the group arrived just before noon, and target practice became instantly postponed when they saw the fish skeleton and skin. The sivilin were gone, but it had been awhile since any of them had caught fish, and even Rhee helped fillet one from the deep pool. Arak's crossbow shot was the center of conversation, and he shared the image several times. The flying monster had disappeared over the pass between Sagitar and Thunder mountain shaking its head. They attributed their good luck to a well placed shot that had nothing to do with a thick double bladed shaft. All of them had seen similar images from battles over the Desowan, and even Arak had to agree.

Target practice that afternoon along the escarpment was uneventful, and they didn't mention a word of the sivilin incident to Orem or Magahila who showed up when they were finished with the fish. They did tell the instructors that two had been sighted. Magahila was worried about the sivilin and she stood watch while effortlessly soaring updrafts and ridge lift along the front of the Thunder mountain summit.

Arak's stunners hit the target every time, and even Shandra hit it a quite a few times out of a couple dozen dives. Enneka was getting better, hitting his mark almost half of the time, and Dulles hit his target more often as did Rhee. Orem took a couple of shots at the student's request, and although he missed the target once the stunner hit the cliff only a couple of inches from the edge of the straw matt.

Rhee was the only one that had trouble loading her bow in the air while falling, and she strained a muscle in her shoulder that caused her some pain, but it was one of Orem's requests. Other than that, and the sivilin attack, the rest of the day was uneventful. The morning's excitement had diminished to a brief encounter for everyone but Arak and Shandra. Finally, Orem signaled from the base of the huge cliff that it was time to head home.

Magahila had dropped from her position as sentry along the mountain front, and she stood beside him. Her single shot at the matt when she'd swooped down in an inverted dive had been low by a couple of feet. They picked up the last of the thick shafted stunners along the base of the cliff, and were only missing three or four out of forty some that they'd brought from the arsenal; and of course the one Arak had dropped before diving on the sivilin.

Orem was amazed at the precision accomplished by Arak, and complimented him again. Arak attributed his skills to the many hours he had spent while his father had coached him in extreme conditions within the Glass canyons. He'd become proficient in ridge soaring and some other basic stunts at the age of five, and he'd only been nine years old when he'd made his first kill. Arak had been practicing with various crossbows since he could remember; even before he could fly.

Miz returned that evening, and Numak's wing or group of hunters had killed a sivilin. They'd also severely wounded a second one, but they hadn't been able to find a second carcass the following day. No one had been hurt, and they carried the sivilin's head into the Sagitarian gorge on three lines. It was placed above the entrance of the main cavern with twenty-five others; some bleached and some that had been more freshly skinned. Black horns jutted backward from all twenty-five skulls in a very impressive and sinister manner. It was Savant's goal to kill a sivilin every week, but they were falling way short. They were usually lucky to get one confirmed kill every couple of weeks. Only four had met their demise in the past two months. The sivilin over the Desowan were hard to find in places where they could be attacked safely, and they were very aggressive.

Savant was still supreme in Sagitar, and his leadership had remained undisputed for over a decade. His incredible ability to send and receive images would probably keep him so until he was very old or perhaps even dead. He was trying to keep a tally on confirmed throat and neck shots that had caused injury by the Sagitarian hunters, and even though the confirmed kill count was low, at least a hundred sivilin had been driven off in the past year. There was always a celebration when a skull was hung on the cliff wall, and tonight would be no exception.

The feast of sorts would start in the glacial cirque at the base of Mount Sagitar where wine and brandies would be poured and consumed. The images of the kill would be projected and shared to all of the colony members of age. The kill had taken several hours, and had transgressed more than a hundred miles, or five hours glide time. Only neural highlights would be projected, but it would probably take at least an hour to watch the telepathic images from four or five individuals who had been in on the kill.

Luckily the event over the Desowan overshadowed Arak's lucky bow shot, and none of the students that had been there mentioned it. Miz sat across from the Sagitarian leader in the main cavern before the meeting in the cirque with Arak and Shandra at the same table. They both witnessed neural images of Arak's marksmanship while diving along the cliff wall, and Savant complimented the young klute on his prowess. He was also impressed by the copies of the ceremonial arrow, and he said that he'd also possessed one at a younger age. He'd placed it with his grandparent's remains at the burial site south of the city.

It was early in the evening, but many of the Sagitarian inhabitants, and sivilin hunting visitors were beginning to arrive with wines, brandies, and foodstuffs. Cooking fires burned at a dozen locations within the gigantic cavern and meals were beginning to be prepared. Freshly killed tusked Horat was the main course for one large group, and there was also chura steak, with wildfowl of various types. Fish was seldom brought into the main cavern, and was almost always prepared on the spot as a shore lunch, but some smoked it. A few of the most talented musicians from Taro began playing stringed and hollow fluted instruments, and an older couple from the Baden River colony joined in with several small different pitched drums.

Arak could tell his mother was having a good time while she drank wine with Savant and Allie. She'd quit worrying about Cin for the time being. Shandra's parents were also present, and they sat with friends at a table right behind Allie. Shandra's mother was helping with the cooking of a buck that had been brought from just north of the Baden River. There were roasts, steaks, and stews cooking at three nearby fires. Arak had opted for a big chura steak cooked on one of the ancient firestone grilles.

Within an hour there were almost three hundred klutes in the cave, and the meals were quickly served. About fifty sivilin hunters ate in the main cavern every night, but it was usually quiet after dark. Tonight the noise of the large group was noticeably accentuated by the music and extra quantities of alcoholic beverages that were being consumed. Savant finally addressed the group and said that Numak was ready to share the images of the sivilin kill. The cavern began emptying out slowly at first, then more quickly with sometimes five or six unfurling their wings at the entrance at the same time.

The bright moon was three quarters above ice on the south side of Tempest mountain when Arak, Shandra, and Miz made their way to the cirque. Everyone sat on flattened granite stones or glacial moraine that littered the level floor of the giant coliseum. At least two dozen small campfires flickered on the floor of the huge amphitheater that had been scooped out generations earlier by an ice floe that had since receded to a small patch of ever present snow that lay most of the way up the shallow canyon between the two granite peaks west of the colony. The peak on the left was called Tempest and the one on the right was called Froze to Death mountain.

Numak and his number one wingman Derek, sat on the eight foot granite rostrum. Numak was sipping from a handled mug, and firelight flickered from two good sized campfires below them, as their legs dangled from the edge. Idle conversation went on concerning the altitudes at which the hunters were finding sivilin. There had been a few sighted at timberline and a half, but not many over the years, and it was starting to become obvious that the winged nemesis was actually restricted to an altitude ceiling far below that of the klutes.

Finally, when everyone was present and more wines and brandies had been passed around Numak began projecting images. The first neural signals involved six hunters and two sivilin in a simultaneous attack. One sivilin ended up with two crossbow bolts in its throat and the other one ended up with an arrow just below its throat and two in its neck.

Miz had been with the second wave of hunters, and after the images of the first attack had been shared throughout the coliseum a couple times Numak summoned her to the podium. She was surprised, but quickly strolled between small fires to the giant rock. The second attack had occurred minutes after the first, and had involved the last three hunters of Numak's group. The images showed Miz and her partners plunging past the sivilin in the preferred inverted dive while firing their arrows into the flying lizards throat.

Arak suddenly became very proud of his mother as the telepathic images began to take form. The sivilin was only a couple thousand feet from the ground on this attack, but its partner or mate had suddenly banked sharply and turned east.

When it was safely out of reach Miz had decided to dive. Her neural images were very clear as they were shared throughout the large group. Her brazen attack was also successful and there were now three arrows imbedded in the sivilin's throat just below its massive lower jaw, and two in its neck. Miz and her two wingmen plummeted toward trees in a deep canyon between two big rusty colored flat topped mesas. She stopped projecting the telepathic signals when the three of them were safely beneath the leafy upper canopy of a forty acre forest surrounding a small lake.

She started projecting again when the enraged sivilin followed them and actually landed in a rocky clearing near the lake. The thing shrieked as it began walking along the edge of the treeline near the lakeshore. It suddenly stopped and began scraping at its throat with the claws of its front feet. This behavior lasted for about five minutes, then the giant lizard flew off with visible blood streaks staining its neck.

Numak began projecting again, and his images portrayed that he had caught a thermal and was already back to about a third timberline. There was no sign of the second reptile so they followed the sivilin northeast for two hours barely able to keep it in sight. Finally the thing began to slow down. Numak let Derek project the images of the next attack when another arrow was driven into the creature's bloody throat and two more into its neck. The first hand memories showed the damage the flying behemoth had sustained. Its whole neck was soaked in blood. It landed on top of a rocky promontory above a wide arid valley that had been wiped clear of vegetation by years of flashfloods. The reptile began clawing at its throat again. The next series of memories were from the following day and portrayed Numak standing on the creature's side as it lay dead at the base of the same rocky mesa near an intermittent stream.

Now that the primary images had been shared by the hunters, others with extraordinary photographic memory recall began re-sharing them to smaller groups throughout the giant natural amphitheater. The images would soon be permanently etched in the memory banks of those that wished. Arak would remember the visions of his mother's perfect shooting and be able to project them quickly to anyone at any time. Many other relatives and friends would be able to relay some of the images that had just been shared for years or perhaps even decades, but over time the memories would fade, especially the colors. They would become fuzzy for all but a few with exceptional recall.

Arak paid special attention to the exact flight of Numak's and his mother's arrows. He would try to imitate the shots as closely as possible even though he had already succeeded in wounding one of the creatures.

The image sharings were a good way to keep everyone motivated even though they knew they were fighting a futile battle against a huge extremely dangerous creature that was wiping out whole herds of mikta and chura across the delta. The invasive species was so powerful and adaptable to different climates and topographical changes that the klutes were afraid it would eventually kill all of the cloven hooved animals on the delta; from there the extinctions would probably spread world wide.

When the sivilin's demise had been shared to everyone's satisfaction scouts began sharing their adventures from the huge boulder; mostly unusual sightings over the Desowan. There were even some images of the strange flat topped mountains beyond the wasteland. The mountains lay about two thirds of the way across the continent, and reached fingers out into a huge lake called Sivilin lake.

The North Desowan river flowed into the lake about three hundred miles from the outlet. Beyond that and farther to the east there was another long wide peninsula stretching for more than a thousand miles south along the eastern ocean but maps in this area were vague. The oceans were named. The western ocean was called the Sagitarian sea, the southern ocean was called the Taro sea and the eastern ocean was called the Desowan ocean. Old scrolls and rituals simply called the eastern ocean 'Land's End', and the scrolls referred to the sea south of Taro as 'South Land's End'. Only a few had ever ventured to the eastern sea, and it was unnamed in scrolls more than two hundred years old.

The red moon was referred to as the night hunter or sometimes even the zinda hunter because the best time to hunt zinda was during the phase while its bright sister was new and on the other side of the world. The big cats were almost a hundred percent nocturnal, hunting only during the darkest hours of the night, and with no moonlight at all they were almost impossible to see; even for a klute. In the winter the northern species turned white to aid in its camouflage. The slightly larger brighter moon was called the chura hunter for the same reason. The best time to hunt the forest for mountain chura was at night when the brighter moon or both moons were full. The herbivores would stray into the open parks or clearings with darkness and begin grazing in the open meadows.

The zinda hunter, or red moon was just rising above the skyline of the Moon creek divide when the klutes departed the amphitheater. Intoxicating effects of the carefully fermented beverages were enhanced by the hypnotic rhythmic sounds of the music created by a half dozen individuals who were gifted in the art, and the celebration went on until well past midnight. Miz let Arak and Shandra each have a mug of her homemade wine after the image sharing. Arak was glad that his accomplishment with the quad bladed ceremonial arrow had gone completely unnoticed.

Magahila or Duroon would punish them irregardless.

CHAPTER FOUR

Cin stood on top of the tallest mountain peak along the eastern edge of the pine forested valley and magnified his vision. He'd spent the night in his hammock beneath the upper canopy in the pleasant forest, and had awakened munching on pine nuts from giant nearby cones. They were plentiful and very easy to forage. He'd found many ways to supplement his diet in the surrounding area over the past few days. Wild fruit bearing trees were even growing around a small spring fed pool about a hundred yards from his campsite. The fruit was of a dark purplish tint with a reddish orange streaking; sort of like the red streaks on the Sagitarian terravine. It wasn't as big as terravine, but very tasty.

There was also another type of tree near the pond that produced a huge black fruit or nut of some kind. He removed the soft porous outer skin and held a nut about the size of a moolarine skull, or a little bigger than his fist. He tried to smash open the thing with a rock but his first attempts were unsuccessful. Finally he was able to remove the shell and it was nice tasting inside but hard to scrape the brown meaty core out of the broken shell. He placed part of it in his pack, then selected a couple more.

Cin finished the last of the wildfowl he'd killed the previous day, then feeling very refreshed after the best sleep he'd had since leaving Sagitar, he rolled his hanging and began exploring along the mountains to the northeast in ridge lift that made it easy for him to ascend to timberline.

He soared the western slopes of the mountain range toward the north all morning and spotted a few mountain chura in the muskegs and moolarine ponds of the backed up snowmelting streams. One was an old bull with antlers at least five feet across. Many of the small swamps and lakes were below timberline surrounded by pines, but there were also dozens of tiny glacial fed pools and lakes in the bare blue and grey granite heights; even on the windy barren plateaus. He was satisfied with his long trek over the polar region, and decided to head for home on the morrow as a strong breeze was steady out of the southwest at about timberline. He knew Miz would be very worried even though they'd talked about doing some solitary long distance flights in the past.

He retraced his path to the south along the eastern front and was surprised to find thorny khiska groves again. The gnarly black twisted briars had taken up residence mixed with tall pines along the whole eastern side of the mountain range to an altitude of about eight thousand feet. A few scrubby pines leaned sideways from the ever present winds at the higher elevations below about ten thousand feet, some with branches on only one side.

He soared the mountains gaining memories and exploring future campsites and shelters all day. Late afternoon found him soaring drainages from high lakes dropping off to the south and east in a cold katabatic wind. He decided to land in a narrow pass when he heard the faint distant barking and howling of a mada pack. He had trouble maintaining his balance for a moment when a gust pummeled the narrow ridge joining the two pyramid shaped peaks on each side of him. The wolf or mada pack was behind him somewhere. Probably not more than a couple of miles below him on the sparsely timbered plateau.

The serrated hog's back above the canyon in front of him dropped off into a staircased abyss of narrow ledges to a good sized lake far below. The vertical distance to the valley floor was so extreme that when the wind pushed him a half step toward the edge of the escarpment he experienced a very rare sense of vertigo for a moment. The sensation was nearly inherent within the klute race, but had almost caused him to unfurl his wings. Cin realized that he was standing on a sheer vertical escarpment higher than that of anything he'd encountered himself, or even witnessed at an image sharing.

The madas had been howling and raising a ruckus that could be heard for a few miles, so Cin soared the ridgelift, and drifted back up over the top of the narrow peak for a closer look. They were feeding on something beside a small lake below timberline, probably a chura. He could count ten. Cin was surprised that there were any herbivores in the surrounding countryside at all, and wondered how many wolf or mada packs or perhaps even packs of flying lizards frequented the area.

He'd seen two different species of miktas and he thought maybe three species of chura, but only very small herds, and always in the forest or in a clearing with nearby cover. He'd encountered a few more bands or herds of the small wooly tusked cliff dwellers also, but he'd left them alone.

There were so many huge khiska groves or thickets in the foothills along the eastern mountain range that their thorny trunks and branches would always offer protection to a grazing species. Cin had hunted tusked horat and miktas in the khiska thickets of the Desowan, but here the briar patches seemed even more extensive stretching to the south for as far as the eye could see with islands of pine groves and thick leafy forests breaking up the symmetry. The madas below him had caught the chura out in an open glade near a grassy bog or muskeg beside the lake.

Cin swooped down from the dizzying heights of the rocky crag on the east side of the mountain range unnoticed by any of the denizens that might attack him. He was alert for flying lizards at all times. He soared the gusty ridge lift southward for twenty more miles as the day waned. He would try to see what had made the faint orange glow on the southern horizon the evening before.

It was very cold at timberline and a half, and he quickly changed his elevation dropping to about three thousand feet above ground level. He flew south along the lake shore until he was beyond the southernmost peak in the mountain range. The rolling hilly country beyond and below him was covered by thick pine forest and thorny khiska thickets with leafy deciduous trees along most of the streams. In places fires had burned out of control clearing the land naturally for hundreds and even thousands of acres in random strange looking patterns or grassy parks with blackened pine and bare bleached dead spires poking upward amidst gigantic boulders of the ancient glacial moraine. He spotted a lone antlered chura bull near a small lake in one of them, but the wary herbivore ran from the mucky blackened muskeg forest into the khiska briars as soon as he approached.

The orange glow had enticed him, and he didn't think it was a forest fire because he hadn't seen any smoke. He soared swiftly onward with the help of the cool katabatic winds flowing down off of the not too distant mountains. Cin flew low, and he could tell that the khiska groves were unlike anything he'd ever seen. The thorny bushes were over fifty feet tall on an average with taller monarchs reaching skyward to almost a hundred feet. Gnarly dark branches grew from the twisted trunks at almost every conceivable angle and direction.

The terrain below was rising slightly toward the west, and the meandering streams were all draining toward the north. He found this unusual, but after his many trips over the oxbow canyons and crevassed drainages of the Desowan he knew anything was possible when it came to erosion within igneous or extinct volcanic formations. The rugged country ahead had definitely been altered and created by lava flows many times in the past.

He spotted several herds within the khiska forests, but the briars and branches were so thick he couldn't discern a species, just movement and noise. The wary herbivores were very elusive, more so than anything he'd encountered in his life on the delta or even in the Desowan. The flying lizards were obviously the apex predator here, unless there were sivilin somewhere around. Cin let his curiosity get the best of him as a brilliant rippling sunset cut the horizon with white searchlight streaks made by the suns piercing rays in the eastern sky.

He swooped down into a muskeg sodden clearing in a small canyon and took a short hike beneath the web of branches. He discovered lush thick grasses beneath the khiska in a forest thriving on the loamy volcanic soil. The tunnel like path that he chose out of the ten or twelve that led to the pond was tramped with fresh tracks made by at least five different species. Narrow paths or game trails tunneled into the briars every ten or twenty yards, and the grass was knee deep between the huge trunks of the dark twisted khiska trees. They were four times the size of any in the Desowan, and the upper canopy of thorny branches and leaves completely blocked the evening sunlight in places causing his pupils to dilate almost to their nocturnal state. Cin felt very uneasy walking in the forest, almost claustrophobic in places where thick undergrowth caused the game trails to converge and become very narrow. There were tracks in the soft earthen soil beneath the khiska that had been made by horat, miktas, chura, and many types of wildfowl.

When he neared the canyon's vertical wall he came out in the open and could see a large cave, but as soon as he crossed a set of huge paw prints with four inch claws he decided he'd done enough exploring on the ground. The tracks in the soft moist black dirt were twice the length of his moccasins, and they weren't made by a zinda. They'd been made by a bront. Cin had seen a few on the delta north of the Glass canyon, but he'd never killed one of the rare bearlike creatures. They were dangerous, but not as predatory as a zinda. The animals were omnivores like the sivilin, and could live for long stretches of time on just grass or leaves, but they would kill when the opportunity presented itself.

The huge pawprints gave Cin the creeps in the small confines of the clearing beneath the cliff. He didn't want to tear a wing trying to fly up between the branches so he loaded and cocked his crossbow while retracing his steps to the muskeg pond. He was soon back in the air, but he'd satisfied his curiosity. At least this part of the khiska forest was teeming with wildlife, and an ecosystem undaunted by a species of five or six foot long flying lizards.

Twilight found him about two hours glide west of the pine valley where he'd spent the previous evening, and he was surprised to see dark silhouettes on the horizon ahead. He guessed they were sivilin, and when he magnified his vision he could see three of them slowly descending toward a high rocky tower or pinnacle that constituted the remains of an extinct volcano.

There were several more of the igneous formations visible from his altitude, and they resembled islands in a sea of khiska to the west. He could see five of the strange gigantic boulder strewn vertical formations. They thrust their towers upward from the thorn forest for several hundred feet giving the landscape an unusual eerie splendor. He continued onward for another fifteen minutes slowly dropping toward the ground.

When Cin was about a thousand feet above the khiska he flew westward. Darkness soon manifested itself and the orange glow in the sky reappeared, but it was farther south than he'd thought. He approached the fire a short time later, and realized that it was different than anything he'd ever seen. Huge clay and shale hills had eroded into crevasses and small canyons and there were no khiska. One of the five hundred foot cliffs had sluffed off and an exposed seam of blackened soil was burning out of control with a fierce intensity. The acrid smell made

Cin's eyes water. The huge coal fire produced very little smoke and was burning itself back into the cliff wall where it would produce another landslide in the future. He'd seen the black seams in the Desowan. The klutes knew the strange black rock and sand would burn, but it was of little use to them because of the acrid fumes it produced. They had no way of making it into a weapon of any sort so they just left it where it lay. Lightning had probably started the fire, but he wasn't sure. He hadn't seen a thunderstorm for days. The nearby forest was charred and blackened for miles.

He flew onward for another hour, and after darkness had fallen he discovered an impact crater that stretched for a mile in diameter, and at least a half mile down. The surrounding landscape was completely barren with ash and white stony debris stretching outwards from ground zero for perhaps half an hour's glide in every direction. He magnified his night vision when curiosity got the best of him and could see where the earth had been turned to glass similar to that of the obsidian cliffs of his home in the Glass Canyon.

Cin wondered what could have caused the huge explosion, and as strange emotions crept into his subconscious mindset he banked to the north. Something from offworld or beyond the sky had definitely caused the blast. It had been caused by some kind of a naturally occurring event that was beyond his reckoning or reasoning, and the place made him uneasy. He'd seen places like it before and had seen shooting stars many times. He knew there were many things that his mind didn't comprehend, and space was one of them. Sometimes he just enjoyed a mug of wild cherry brandy while looking up at the stars and the auroras.

He explored the region for over a week and one morning the wind was strong out of the southwest when he rose from his campsite. He would miss the brief stay in the lush forest and its bounty of fruits and nuts, but he could always return someday, and maybe bring Miz, or even a larger group from Sagitar. The place might be a safe haven from the sivilin, and he'd noticed some fairly deep roomy caves along both the east and west slopes of the mountains far-ther to the north in a vertical layer of exposed lime-stone. He'd been disappointed with the absence of any geothermal springs, but that didn't mean there weren't some around somewhere.

Cin was flying beneath a high broken cloud ceil-ing a few days later when he spotted more of the fly-ing lizards. This time they were fighting. It looked like two packs had merged on the same kill and the battle was fierce. He magnified his vision and no-ticed that the carcass of the chura was torn apart and partially devoured; then he also spotted the bodies of two dead madas within a stone's throw of the dead herbivore.

As the battle in the sky below him raged he pulled himself up through a break in the clouds unnoticed. There were at least thirty of the fanged lizards, and though their acrobatics and aerial maneuvers were similar in comparison to a six year old klute, they would be a formidable foe in such great numbers if he were caught off guard. He watched them through a wide break in the cloud as he flew slowly northward and realized that he would be able to outrun them if need be, and he also decided that though the lizards were probably the third most dangerous predator on this continent, they were their own worst enemy. They were killing each other at an alarming rate. They were grappling, snarling, tearing and clawing each other until several of them plummeted to their deaths. He didn't know why; there seemed to be plenty of wild game to go around.

Cin flew onward utilizing the wind to his best ability. He used thermals from the warm summer sunlight during the day and sometimes katabatic evening flows after dark. Some of the thermals would carry him up to an altitude of at least twenty thousand feet, and he would be able to glide northward losing altitude gradually until he found another one. His unique photographic memory allowed him to recognize certain landmarks in an almost uncanny manner, and at night he directed his flight toward the Polaris above the tail of the zinda constellation. He was drifting northward just below a broken cloud ceiling one evening when he noticed something very disturbing. The tiny dots in the distance didn't look like the predators that he'd been encountering, they were too big. They were sivilin, and when Cin magnified his vision he could count nine. The giant reptiles were flying toward the west, and he lost sight of them a few minutes later. He decided to leave well enough alone, and stayed his course. He knew there were sivilin here but not near as many as there were in the Desowan.

Cin slept whenever he became tired; day or night, but usually for only a few hours at a time, until he reached the arctic sea. He searched along the coast for a full day toward the east until he found a familiar secluded rocky outcropping where he could rest for another full day.

Crossing the sea was another story all in itself. Cin drifted for a day, and a night, before he knew he was off course. Either that or there was a bay stretching toward the south just to the east of where he'd transgressed the polar ice cap a month earlier. Maybe he'd been in some kind of upper air flow that had blown him slightly to the east; or perhaps even west. He could see why no one had ever explored the northern region with much success.

The sea ice looked almost the same from more than timberline and a half with very few distinguishable landmarks. For some reason he had lost memory of the scores of islands he'd flown over and he'd drifted off course, but he'd been over cloud part of the time so it was hard to retrace his flight exactly.

Sometimes he could detect shadows against the glare of the continuous sunlight, but mostly it was a white sheen with very few cracks. On the second day he drifted over a thick frontal system and could see nothing but cloud. He was worried, but decided to continue onward with the upper flow at what he guessed was about eighteen thousand feet. He became slightly lightheaded at times and knew he was using hyperoxygenated blood. The sun still circled the horizon never setting, but he could tell it was beginning to dip slightly lower in one place, and he knew this was north so he kept the lowest dip exactly behind him. He hoped he was still going the right way and hadn't deviated his course while crossing the polar cap. Cin dropped through the cloud twice and rested but the weather was cold and windy with sleet. He was still over a white blanket of fog on the morning of his third day after leaving the rocky outcropping at the pole. He could see down through openings at times and could tell that the ice was breaking up.

The sun had dipped below the horizon that evening before coming back up slightly behind him, and he knew he was still going straight south. He was very tired and having trouble maintaining a locked wingspan. Cartilage and tendons were stretched to the limits of their endurance, and muscles were becoming weaker and weaker. He finally gave up and spiraled downward again into the clouds and the unknown. If he was over an ocean without ice he would probably be doomed, and would have to climb back to at least timberline. His food and water supplies were almost depleted and he needed more rest.

CHAPTER FIVE

Arak led the way around Thunder Mountain with Shandra and Enneka right behind. The colony was under a very rare attack, but not by sivilin. It was now past midsummer, and the flu like symptoms had begun popping up in the mortar, adobe, and stone households within the main cavern three weeks previous.

Rhee was very ill and hadn't eaten for two days, and Dulles said he was having trouble sleeping because of a sore throat. Miz had also succumbed to the rampant virus and was weak and in bed with a fever. Over half of the Sagitarian colony was ill, and only a few sorties of sivilin hunters were out over the

Desowan. The blame was on some visitors from the Mocktaw Islands, but Taro was having an epidemic at the same time, and all of the colonies were now exposed so it was hard to say where it had originated. Two deaths had even been attributed to the illness in Sagitar. One infant and one elderly.

They thermalled up on the west slope of Thunder, and rose to almost timberline and a half. The three youngsters still weren't supposed to soar over the Desowan, but hunting wild game was lousy anywhere close to Sagitar, and they were bored. They decided to look for horat in khiska thickets of several nearby canyons just east of the sand hills. Magahila was incapacitated and in bed, as was most of Enneka's family. Shandra's parents had come back from scouting the previous evening and they were both also coming down with colds.

No one would know where the three students were hunting, and that was dangerous, but they hadn't given it a thought. They'd told Orem they were going hunting at breakfast, but they didn't say where. He said he wasn't feeling so well himself, and Duroon was so involved with the sick that he didn't have time to worry about matters such as who was hunting what or where.

"Up there looks the best." Enneka pointed toward a wide mouthed canyon to the north that was choked full of pine encompassed leafy green kishka thickets. The place was marked on one of the giant charcoal maps inscribed on the wall of the main cavern but Arak couldn't remember the name. The young klutes weren't required to know anything about the lands east of the Sagitarian mountain peaks yet, and when they did begin to hunt over the Desowan they would be with experienced hunters and scouts.

The maps of the Desowan on the wall near the stairs into the main cavern were only supposed to be for refreshing sivilin hunters on the territories and canyons east of the mountains. This reverse psychology made it more desirable for the younger generations to memorize the drawings or pictographs. Most of the students in the graduating class wanted to be sivilin hunters someday, and they were very familiar with the Desowan maps. Arak had them memorized in fairly good detail.

They used their wings to pull them northward along with the weak upper air flow and less than an hour later they began circling downward into one of the shallower Desowan canyons.

"It's too thick here." Shandra glanced at Arak, and he pointed to a side channel that had received a lightning strike a few years previous. Most of the north slope had burned, and it was easy to see through the blackened briars and bare pine branches. A few horat were down near the bottom end, and Enneka killed one with his first shot from about thirty yards directly above. The three of them set to work. They laughed and joked, despite the impending doom that had been wrought onto the Sagitarian colony. They all knew that there was probably some kind of higher power that they didn't understand, or maybe another higher plane of existence, and they knew that whatever it was it usually made everything all right in time. This was simply the way the klute mindset worked in stressful situations.

In less than two hours the animal was boned, packed, and ready for transport.

"Why is it so dry out here along the east front?" Shandra looked around at the sandy rocky soil in the burned canyon.

"There's a spring down below I think. It's marked on Savant's map in the main cavern." Arak answered her as he shrugged into his pack. He let her straighten it for him before he tied the straps. He began unfolding his wings, and they followed him as he jogged a few steps into a light breeze before lifting off. In a few moments they were above the tree tops. When they reached the lower canyon they landed and washed the blood from their hands in a long pool of the intermittent stream. It was hot and the creek was surrounded and lined by an odd outcropping of reddish brown and grey splotched sandstone boulders. The rock seemed to reflect the sun but the fresh water coming out of the ground was ice cold.

Arak saw the giant shadows cross a clearing on the nearby barren hillside just across the stream before he looked up, and knew they were sivilin. He could see three of them gliding less than five hundred feet above the canyon either hunting or looking for easy grazing. He put his finger to his lips and pointed upward.

"Shhhh! sivilin!" Arak spoke just loud enough for the others to hear.

Shandra had to stifle an exclamation of surprise and pulled her braids aside so she could get a clear view of the giant apex killers directly above them. Luckily they were unnoticed and they slowly backed away from the pool. They hid in the shadows of a mixed grove made up of stubby pines, leafy saplings, and thorny khiska. The sivilin passed quickly and silently overhead then began climbing toward the mountains. They were even hard to see at a close distance with their blended camouflage patterns. They were so close that Arak could tell that one of them had part of a wing tip missing and another had a hole in one of its wings. He wondered if they fought amongst themselves.

"Looks like they're going to go north of Thunder mountain." Enneka sat down in sparse green grass and leaned against a tree, his pointed wing tips touching the sandy soil. "We might as well wait until they are out of sight. I've never seen them so low except for when we were chased."

When Arak removed his pack and pulled out a lystroot and a couple of sun ripened purple and yellow striped terrafruit Shandra followed suit. She didn't have any fruit so Arak handed her one of his. They watched the sivilin recede into the distance.

"Well I'm just glad for one thing." Said Arak with a grin.

"What?" Queried Shandra. She had her mouth half full of fruit.

Arak laughed. "I'm glad none of them had to poop."

The comment raised a hail of laughter from Enneka and Shandra even though the whole colony might be in danger from the impending virus and encroaching sivilin.

Shandra tried to punch him in the shoulder. "Only you would think of something that stupid to say." She was still laughing as he dodged her harmless blow.

When the low flying sivilin finally gained enough altitude and disappeared over the eastern front north of Thunder mountain the three young klutes headed for the pass on the opposite side.

They deposited the horat meat in the main cavern and found Duroon at one of the cooking fires.

He was administering herbal teas and powdered remedies to a few of the ill that resided in the internal walled dwellings of the main caveran. He said that the virus was becoming even more rampant in the colony, and was glad that the group had found some wild game. Other hunters and scouts were trickling in from west of the Moon Creek drainage, and some had been successful, but most were empty handed. None of them had been hunting in the Desowan, but those with wild game had miktas and spoon billed chilkut from the Moon Creek valley. Landwalkers had domesticated the chilkut and kept them in their villages, but the humans were unable to stalk and kill wild game with the expertise or finesse of the klutes, and the winged race preferred iktar eggs to those of the larger fowl anyway.

Miz said she was feeling a little better when Arak went for a visit, but that's what she always said. Duroon appeared in the open doorway of the small cave while they were cooking fresh horat loin in the fireplace near the entrance. She ate a few bites of the loin in a broth and coughed a few times while she picked at a bowl of terrafruit mixed with greens and herbs. Duroon spiced it up with some medicinal herbs of his own, and she tried to eat the whole bowl before laying back on her low slung fur lined hanging or hammock. She insisted on staying at home. She said the main cavern was too drafty and she didn't really need anybody to look after her anyway. Her fever was almost gone and she was just having respiratory problems.

Mid-afternoon found the three youngsters soaring Mount Sagitar for the second time. Modest west winds were blowing in and Arak banked into a thermal that took him way him up above the south side. The rocky snow streaked peaks stretched to the southern horizon branching out into the Desowan and west to the Sagitarian River gorge. The highest one was called Skree mountain, and it was still streaked with deep snowfields. Enneka was below him and Shandra was in another warm rising thermal just to the south when Enneka pointed out over the Desowan.

"That's a sivilin down there over the sand hills."

Arak magnified his vision and could see the creature gliding down from the mountains toward the Desowan at about three quarters timberline. It was alone for some reason and he suddenly became excited. It was high enough for an attack and in a perfect spot. The brush and pine filled canyons beyond the sand dunes would make for good hiding if the thing chased them.

"What do you think? Should we see if we can get over top of it?"

Enneka looked at him and grinned. "Yeah. Let's try to hit it with some of your quad bladed arrows and hide in the kishka canyons till dark."

Shandra was still out of earshot, but she was coming up fast. Arak sent her an image and motioned for her to hurry, then he pointed at the sivilin about two miles distant.

"I see it now." She squinted as she magnified her vision then shook her head when the other two began to bank toward it. "We've already done more flying in the Desowan than anybody else our age since the beginning of time. You can't seriously be thinking of an attack."

Arak handed a quad blade to Enneka and looked back at Shandra. "Come on; it's a perfect set up." They'd all modified their bows and he reached in his quiver and pulled out a couple more arrows before finding another of his homemade ceremonial points. He handed it to her. "Just do like we did the last time but aim higher."

She shook her head again and looked at him wide eyed. "If one of us gets killed it will be a hard thing to think about for the rest of our lives."

Enneka swiveled his head and glanced back at her. "Almost everybody is sick, some are dying, and some are probably being attacked and maybe even killed somewhere by sivilin right now. If you want to go back nobody is stopping you."

The three of them closed the distance quickly, and soon they began their silent inverted descent.

They dropped swiftly past the sivilin at about a fourth terminal velocity and as usual it raised its head and pulled up slightly as if startled. Arak's arrow went into the sivilin's throat almost perfectly, and Shandra's was only a foot lower, with Enneka's a couple feet below that. All three of the arrows hit the thing in the throat and upper neck penetrating to their hilts, and the flying monster let out an enraged shriek that Arak would never forget as he folded his wings.

The three of them dove recklessly as fast as they could toward the kishka canyon and the enraged sivilin followed, but it was much too slow. The rushing wind at terminal velocity made verbal communication almost impossible, so Arak squinted through his watery eyes and looked at a small opening in the tangled brushy canyon almost directly below and sent the image to the others. The seconds ticked by, and soon they were even with the walls of the steep sided canyon. Arak noticed that the sivilin was pulling out of its dive well above the shallow rim when he unfurled his wings. The three of them were flaring for a landing in the tiny clearing when Enneka began laughing hysterically.

"Nothing to it!" He laughed gleefully. "Sivilin hunting is almost as easy as gathering iktar eggs."

"The ceremonial points are very accurate." Shandra laughed along with Enneka, but Arak was still watching the sivilin. It was circling as if beginning a slow descent while clawing at its neck with one of its forelegs. It rolled to the side for a moment, and slipped rapidly toward the canyon while scraping at the arrows with its claws. Arak magnified his vision, but the sivilin was moving so fast he had trouble focusing. He could tell there was blood oozing from the wounds but not how much, and it was shrieking and gliding down toward them at an alarming rate again.

"Come on!" He shouted. "We're not out of danger yet!"

They quickly followed him into the gloomy leafy shadows of the tallest saplings and pine trees, then hid alongside the edge of a big thicket where they could take flight again if necessary. A sivilin might still be able to get them if it was persistent, but some of the pine trees were well over a hundred feet tall with long branches more than a foot in diameter, and the klutes would be able to gain distance within the forest at any time with their superior maneuverability.

It was a hot summer afternoon, and it felt good to sit in the shade. Arak chose a mossy boulder as his seat and peered back through the foliage but there was no sign of the huge winged lizard. He could still feel his heart beating from the adrenaline rush. The thing had gone down somewhere along the edge of the canyon wall about a half mile from them and there was no sign of it.

"How long do you want to wait?" asked Shandra. The small Desowan forest in the shallow steep sided canyon was mysteriously silent with very few bird or animal noises. The only sound was the trickling of a tiny stream.

Arak looked at her for a moment before shrugging his shoulders. "We're in no hurry and it will be dark in a couple hours." He looked at her seriously. "You are right you know. The quad bladed arrows are much more accurate in the wind. The flat single points of the other arrows almost always seem to cause them to deviate and veer off course slightly whichever way they angle into the wind."

Enneka began shrugging out of his pack, but Arak walked back into the trees toward the rocky wall of the canyon for a short distance before removing his. The rock cliff was almost vertical, but there were no caves, shelters, or overhangs anywhere nearby. When he sat down with his back to a tree about a hundred yards from Enneka, Shandra joined him. They watched and waited patiently until it was almost dark. The forest had sprung to life gradually with some songbirds and even a couple of flying moolara chit chitting and running and gliding around in the upper branches. There were even some tiny furred spotted sprites darting from tree to tree perhaps wondering what sort of strangers or demons were invading their domain.

There continued to be no sign of the sivilin. Either it had flown off somewhere, or it was on the ground. Perhaps it was injured very badly.

Both of the moons would rise with the sunset, and they were almost in full phase, but they wouldn't rise for a couple of hours because of the nearby mountain range. They continued to wait, but there was only silence in the coming darkness. Arak decided to stay a bit longer just to be sure they would be able to elude the creature, even though they might get in trouble with Magahila. Sivilin seldom ever flew at night, but they'd been seen at half timberline at times over the Desowan when both moons were shining at half or more.

"Magahila is going to be really mad." Said Shandra. "I would almost rather take my chances with the wounded sivilin than get on her bad side again."

"She is really sick. I don't think we have anything to worry about. Enneka is the only one that ever got her and Duroon's full-fledged punishment. If it wasn't for Orem being from the Glass Canyon Shandra and I would have gotten the same terrible treatment." Arak laughed. "You guys looked miserable waiting on tables dishing out food for the younger class, and Rhee looked very shameful when cleaning all of the latrines every day while one of the grounded elders watched. I think she even had to clean the chalow pens."

"It was a good idea to steal a few from the land-walkers, but I don't think anyone likes the stinky chalow pens; especially in the winter. Those little things can pee more than a full grown chura bull." Shandra laughed along with the other two. "Orem's punishment is always more practical." She glanced quickly up through the branches when a loner maul gliding past over-head made a familiar sounding call, perhaps out of curiosity or maybe to warn others of its kind that there were trespassers in the forest. "Sometimes he just sends someone to the gardeners to help till or plant the soil outside of the main cave, or help prune fruit trees or bushes.

Domesticated inbred chalows were actually a very clean animal to keep in captivity with droppings similar to that of a mikta, and they could forage for themselves on the steppes most of the time; even in the winter. They were almost as hardy as a herd of miktas, but some of the taller grasses on the higher elevations to the west of Sagitar were cut and stockpiled for the milking females.

"It was my idea to circle Thunder and go over the sand hills that day; but when Sentell's group of sivilin hunters saw us they made sure everybody knew where we were." Enneka was polishing his bow with the sleeve of his thin skinned jacket. "Magahila kind of made an example of me. I think the worst punishment except for cleaning latrines is helping some of the handicapped get around."

"Yeah. Me to." Arak looked at him. "Except for the sivilin hunters. They're fun to visit with and they share images that they're not supposed to. I've seen some of Himal's. He showed me a few restricted memories one day when I helped him move some stuff."

"I don't know how he can walk on that leg." Shandra spoke up. "It's bent like my bow and his foot is turned almost sideways. I don't know how he survived."

"He's tough." Enneka laughed. "Too bad he lost the use of his left wing, but I think he's happy, and he does have some of the most unique visions to share. Especially when he has had too much wine to drink."

It was very quiet in the small secluded canyon again when nobody spoke for a minute. Not hardly even a breeze rustled the leaves. There were just a few birds or insects chirping.

"I think we can go now." Arak walked to the center of the tiny clearing and scanned the sky. "I'll go up for a look. If it's clear I'll send you an image of the mountains."

"Shandra and Enneka both nodded their agreement and Arak spread his wings. As soon as he was above the trees he headed for the upper east slopes.

The mountains were dark rose colored with the sunset, and they dwarfed the darker countryside. There was no sign of the wounded sivilin so he sent the other two a neural signal. Several minutes later he was a few thousand feet above the eastern foothills of the Desowan.

They joined him near timberline a short time later, and in the last rays of twilight they rose up to the snowline and through Thunder pass.

The next morning Miz was having a slight relapse, and the illness had spread throughout the colony to almost every family within the cliff dwellings or caves. The open floor of the main cavern was littered with the sick. Just a few individuals were working around the cooking fires.

Savant held a short meeting and instructed everyone to remain in Sagitar. No sorties were to go out over the Desowan, and anyone that was up and healthy was expected to remain in the colony to help with the sick if possible. The disease had many side effects, and one of the most disturbing was partial or even complete loss of imaging skills after the fever had manifested itself.

Duroon seemed inexhaustible; instructing and leading small groups, sharing his herbal healing and fever reduction remedies. Arak, Shandra, and Enneka all flew up to the Sagitarian glaciers and brought back ice for those with high fevers. For some reason the three of them were still completely healthy, but there had been a virus go through the colony the previous fall and they'd been slightly ill, so they might have acquired a resistance to a similar strain.

The three of them were sitting in the academy having breakfast; the sun was just rising. Shades of blended pinks, and oranges lit a few high wispy cirrus clouds that were latticed above the immense Sagitarian canyon.

Two young females approached their table with drinks, fruit, and stacks of lysocakes slathered with terravine syrup. They'd chosen a table by the doorway, and a sudden cold breeze caused Shandra to tie the front of her carefully tailored lightweight zinda fur jacket. Her dark semi translucent wings were stretched out slightly behind her with the tips just resting on the floor in a usual fashion. Arak could see that she'd been to the hot springs the evening before, and he could smell scented oils that had been brought from the Baden river colony.

"Everyone is getting the fever." Enneka speared a couple of cakes from the platter and began slicing them into wedges. Arak looked down at the river and discerned the colony's dozen or so stone and adobe storage sheds below. He realized that his friend was right. There was no activity in the colony at all. It was almost as if everyone was gone. Even the main cavern seemed quiet with everyone resting. Only one cooking fire was visible.

"My mom's been eating a little bit, and she can drink chalow milk. Duroon says she should be better by now though." Arak spoke as he scooped another spoonful of berries from a bowl that had been placed in front of him. He took a bite from a syrup laced lystocake.

Arak, Shandra, and Enneka finished their meal and after they gathered all of their weapons they headed for the pass along mount Sagitar. The three students were rising along the side of the mountain in a weak thermal when suddenly a piercing shriek cut through the cool quiet morning air.

It was definitely a sivilin and it was in or directly over the Sagitarian canyon somewhere south of them. There hadn't been many sivilin seen in the canyon this close to the colony. The sivilin hunters were usually able to turn them back in the Desowan. Arak banked into a tight turn and scanned the horizon. He finally spotted three of the giant flying lizards coming up the river from somewhere south of Skree mountain. The light cerulean blue and grey camouflaged splotchy hides were barely discernable against the hazy early morning mist rising from the river. They were flying slowly up the canyon at about timberline. Suddenly one of them banked down toward the klute city and began losing altitude. The other two sivilin just rose up over the plateau about two miles in front of them and drifted out toward the Desowan.

Shandra was flying beside him now and she watched in silence for a moment.

"Let's go." Arak said suddenly, and he motioned for Enneka and Shandra to follow as he quickly pulled a crossbow bolt from his quiver.

They flew swiftly southward next to the cliff wall trying not to attract attention, and when they were a couple of miles south of mount Sagitar they'd already risen into sunlight above the shadows of the western rim. When they reached three quarters timberline they were across the river and heading back toward the city. The sivilin that had dropped toward the colony was out of sight behind the jagged granite ridge that slanted from the steppes to the southwest. Hopefully it had flown out of the canyon, but Arak realized that it could be on the ground. The projecting ridge and cliff housed the main cavern, and if the sivilin was on the ground it was probably already in the chalow pens getting an easy meal.

"Where did it go?" Shandra was just to his left and she was also looking back. Enneka was slightly behind and above both of them. "I don't see it anywhere yet." He said.

"Hurry!" Arak shouted. "I think it has gone all of the way down into the canyon."

Miz heard the sivilin's unmistakable shriek, and sat bolt upright on her hammock in the upper cave that served as their small family alcove. She was sweating and slightly dizzy with fever as she pulled the awning aside peering out. She could see a sivilin descending quickly toward the chalow pens and watched helplessly. It was straight east across the canyon from the main cooking cavern, and just above the pens. Too weak to fly she could only hope for the best. Chalows could be replaced, and luckily it was early enough that not many klutes were out and about performing tasks such as cultivating terravine, lysoroot, or searching for medicinal herbs or other foods along the mountainsides. She could see someone near the pens and became alarmed. The chalows were herded onto the upper meadows every day after milk was taken. This was one of the first tasks for a few of the the colony's inhabitants every morning.

Miz watched helplessy as the chalow herder tried to hide in the shadows behind a depleted winter grassy stockpile.

Only a few dozen of the klutes were able to move about due to the seriousness of the illness, and the sivilin was completely unaware of any other presence when Savant and Duroon ushered everyone within the cave into the deeper shadows and out of sight. The thing was focused on the easy prey in the chalow pens.

It was a cool morning and fruit trees that had been planted in the gardens along the front of the cave blocked its view along with steam rising from the small geothermal hot springs. Several of the klutes in the main cavern readied their crossbows. They were unaware that anyone was outside near the chalow pens.

The sivilin landed dexterously on slender but very strong legs, and its two and three foot long claws scratched ruts in the sod and gravel as it came to a stop near the chalow pens. It whipped its tail around nervously as it surveyed the surrounding area, then it knocked a small pole fence over near the rock walled enclosure. It saw the caretaker behind the haystack and lunged forward like a viper striking its prey. The chalow herder never had a chance and died within seconds, her body nearly torn in half. The sivilin sniffed and pawed at the corpse with its claws as if confused or disturbed about the leather clothing or something, then turned and lunged for one of the fattest grey and white spotted chalows. About fifteen of the goatlike animals were huddled against the cliff wall in the fence corner.

Two foot fangs protruded offensively from the sivilin's stinking massive maw, and the chalow bleated for a moment, its last breaths. The sivilin ambled casually away from the rock wall and walked over the disheveled fence before unfolding giant wings.

It was soon in the air circling upward out of the box canyon toward the river and Mount Sagitar's craggy nearly vertical sunny slopes. Perhaps it was instinct or maybe the creature actually knew there would be warmer air on that side of the canyon. Soon it was at three quarters timberline, and it continued circling leisurely in a warm column of rising air. The limp lifeless prey was hanging from its nearly closed jaws.

Miz was heartbroken for whoever had been watching the chalow pens. She knew most of the herders but wasn't sure which one it was. Some of them were like Nooney and unable to fly, but they could stroll up behind the main cavern past some of the hot springs on a path that led up into the steppes. So many were sick that she wasn't sure who was helping who with the chores.

She watched the sivilin gain altitude until it was about five thousand feet above her vantage point, then something else suddenly caught her attention. She tried to magnify her vision but it just became blurry due to her fever. She watched as three tiny specks dropped into the canyon. They were falling at what appeared a dangerous speed for flying so close to the cliff wall, and they were closing in on the sivilin.

The huge flying lizard was completely unaware of their presence, and raised its head slightly as if startled when they flashed past unleashing their arrows.

Miz knew they were experienced sivilin hunters. The giant winged creature shrieked and banked to the south at an eighty degree angle following the klutes, then it began shaking its head violently. It shrieked again, then leveled off and began gaining altitude. Suddenly the lifeless chalow fell from its mouth, rolling, somersaulting, and tumbling toward the rocks far below. The sivilin was in extreme distress and continued clawing at its throat and lengthy neck while trying to fly with its head turned back at times.

The enormous winged creature gained altitude swiftly. It flew up over the eastern rim along Thunder mountain and disappeared. There was a sudden grim realization that the luxurious Sagitarian lifestyle was in jeopardy. It had been centuries since the archives had recorded a sivilin attacking a klute or a landwalker colony. Miz was relieved to see the three hunters drift off to the south unscathed, and she leaned back in her hammock exhausted from just standing and watching for a few minutes.

Arak, Shandra, and Enneka had all connected with their arrows, but they were dangerously close to the cliff wall, and rising thermals were making the air unpredictable. The giant reptile banked to follow them, and Arak fought to stay away from the rock face while maintaining a dive at a speed near terminal velocity. He could see Shandra to his right and slightly above, and she was also dangerously close to the wall. Enneka had drifted out aways, and was plummeting headfirst toward the valley floor.

Suddenly the frustrated sivilin broke off the attack, and while shaking its head violently the monster dropped the dead chalow and began shrieking. At least one of the arrows had hit a sensitive place or nerve in the creature's neck or throat, and it was furious. When the sivilin leveled off and began to fly out of the canyon Arak and Shandra slowed their descent and banked carefully away from the cliff.

CHAPTER SIX

Cin circled bravely downward through the cloud not knowing what was below, and a feeling of elation coursed through his veins when he could suddenly see land beneath the murky dark grey ceiling. At first it was hard to tell how high he was but he magnified his vision slightly and depth perception gradually showed that he was at about two thousand feet. He continued his descent while watching for signs of sheltered or timbered valleys, but excitement gradually turned to disappointment with the nearly complete absence of vegetation.

The landscape below him was bleak, inhospitable, and barren. Black and grey granite stretched for as far as he could see in every direction polished by eons of erosion and glaciers. There were serrated ridges and crevasses however, and he soon picked a thick brushy spot beneath one of the serrated ridges as a resting place.

There was a crack with an overhanging ledge beneath a huge rocky projection that jutted upwards for about five hundred feet. The projection was split in two places halfway up, and resembled three fingers of a giant hand at the top. He was out of the wind and misty rain, and soon sparked a nice fire with dry wood, grass, and moss under a slight overhang on the lee side below the western inland finger. Cin was glad he hadn't foolishly thrown away any of his supplies, and while resting and relaxing his tired muscles he ate a good size chunk of cooked meat that he'd soaked in sea salt and brought along.

There was a place for his hammock, and when he was fairly sure he was safe from predators he slept through the night without stirring. He rested for a few days while exploring his surroundings, and pillaged a few nesting gulls and iktars of their freshly lain eggs along the coast. On the evening of the third day he rose into a moonlit night beneath a rare clear sky, and drifted south along the western edge of a wide peninsula.

Cin was glad he could see the stars again, but slightly disturbed. His excursion over the clouds had taken him farther south than he'd predicted. He hadn't realized how far south he'd drifted. The Zinda constellation was almost directly above him now.

He flew further south for most of the night letting the inconsistent trade winds take him when possible, and when the peninsula ended he cut across the sea toward a coastline to the west just visible on the horizon from timberline and a half.

He was using hyperoxygenated blood part of the time and dropping to timberline once in awhile to replenish his supply of stored oxygen. The upper stream of air was much faster at the higher altitude. He guessed that sometimes he was traveling at a speed that he'd only surpassed in gusts when dropping down off of Mount Sagitar ahead of strong storms. When the sun finally rose to his right he was over land again. There were a few icebergs in the ocean below, but the sea was open and crystal clear. He decided to spend a day resting after doing some morning hunting.

The sea malara were plentiful on one of the larger icebergs and he could see spray spouting from the blowholes of some nearby whales. There were two pods of unusual grey and white spotted whales near the coastline. The fifty foot long mammals didn't look like anything that he'd seen along the west coast and they were only about half the size. Cin flew for a closer look so he would be able to share the memories someday.

He shot a malara through the heart with his crossbow as it lay resting on its side near the center of one of the flatter chunks of ice. Cin quickly removed the backstraps and some of the long muscles of the hind quarters, then after wrapping them in part of the hide he placed them in his pack. He left the carcass on the ice for the iktars and gulls and headed for shore. He assumed and hoped that it was the mainland. There were cliffs along the coast, sometimes reaching upwards for five hundred feet or more, and he drifted over and down into a pine forested land with very few leafy trees or deciduous forest of any kind.

He cut the meat into thin strips with his razor sharp obsidian knife, and using damp wood on top of a hot fire he began smoking the backstraps and hind quarters on a triple frame braced pole. After he had everything set up he constructed a crude pine bough shelter around his fire and meat pole to keep the smoke and some of the heat in. He stayed in the rainforest for two days. It was cold at night and the weather made a turn for the worse but he was an expert at weaving pine boughs and stayed dry in his hammock under a thick canopy about thirty feet up the west side of a huge evergreen. With his pack full of smoked dried malara he continued his journey south along the coast.

He was lucky and an extremely rapid southerly flow continued along the coastline at about fifteen thousand feet. Cin saw his first sivilin a few days after he left the site where he'd smoked the meat. It was a big one and was flying south also, but it was way below him and unaware of his presence. It was following the coastline perhaps looking for malara or some other prey along he rocky windswept beaches. He banked right and gave the huge flying nemesis a wide berth before continuing southward. The prevailing winds changed from the north to north east, and he was still able to soar rapidly southward with very little effort but it became overcast so he had to drop below the clouds. He didn't want to drift over the sea and get lost again. The cold intermittent rain coming from a ceiling of about half timberline was miserable.

As the days progressed the weather broke and the sun even began peeking through. It was much warmer at his present latitude, and he saw snowy mountains to the south rising along the coast. He was surprised to see three more sivilin below him soaring the beaches. Cin used his extraordinary vision and squinted at times to magnify the broken rocky and sandy beaches below. There were no malara at all and he guessed the sivilin were killing anything offering easy prey. He camped in forest a few miles inland along a stream and killed a large flying moolara with his crossbow. He skinned the animal and skewered the whole carcass after removing the entrails. It sizzled on a rotisserie over a crackling fire a short time later.

The closer Cin got to the mountain range the more sivilin he saw. The sky was clear and he counted seven of the flying reptiles the next day. The never ending gloomy weather and rain seemed to finally be ending as he soared into the southern latitudes of the continent. Eluding sivilin was becoming monotonous so he rose to an altitude somewhere around timberline and a half and began using hyperoxygenated blood. He drifted inland using thermals along with a slight westward airflow and soared above more mountains that afternoon. There weren't as many sivilin inland but he did see two of the giant flying scourge when he dropped down off the west slopes toward a long lake. There were more snowy peaks on the western horizon beyond the lake and foothills, and they looked extremely rugged in places with gigantic pointy pillars stretching to the heavens at a height that appeared almost twice timberline. It was another rare sunny day and he was sure that the clean virgin snow layering the upper halves of the peaks were seeing their first rays of sunlight.

Cin noticed fish running up the wide stream between the lake and the ocean, and he dropped to the forest floor. There were thousands of good sized silver and red streaked fish spawning and he set to work. He made a triple pronged spear out of a sturdy seven foot long willow, and enjoyed fresh fish over the fire that evening saving his supply of smoked malara. The fish were more slender than their western ocean dwelling cousins, and had a much more fearsome set of teeth. They also had longer fins. They were a welcome respite from his usual diet.

A long canyon running east and west split the peaks along the coastline as he continued onward the next morning above a marine layer of fog, and he followed it inland for a while. There were more sivilin here. The place seemed to be crawling with them. The igneous volcanic cliffs along the canyon's edge were a couple thousand feet high and they were pock marked with caves and overhanging ledges. Every cave seemed to be a lair for one or more of the winged beasts. Cin landed at one high overlook and stood brazenly near the edge of a two thousand foot drop. The wind ruffled his hair and pushed him backward half a step. He squinted and magnified his vision. He could count twenty seven sivilin. There were sivilin of all sizes from tiny newly hatched to giant grandparents or perhaps ancient great grandparents with wingspans of almost a hundred fifty feet. No one was sure how long a sivilin lived.

The place gave him the creeps and he decided to try to climb out over the massive mountain range to the west and leave it far behind. He flew back northwest parallel to the rim of the canyon staying a couple miles from the edge until he was near the entrance to the mountain range, then he settled in for the night in a forest of giant pines. He snacked on jerky and slept about four hours before taking flight in the darkness. The silver moon or chura hunter was waxing at about three quarters.

He knew sivilin only hunted during the daylight hours over the Desowan, and hoped that was true for this area. Some of the elders in the Taro colony had scrolls dating back four generations that stated sivilin needed sunlight on a regular basis to survive. There were no faded images associated with scrolls dating back this far but the crude writings of the klute race had survived very well. The scrolls also stated that during dismal weather that lasted for long periods groups of sivilin could sometimes be seen on the higher mountain tops basking in the sunlight. The particular scroll had been written during a dangerous time when more sivilin had seemed to invade the klute's homelands on the delta between Sagitar, Taro, and The Glass Canyon.

Cin brazenly flew up the canyon in the darkness, knowing that there were probably sivilin all around him sleeping in their lairs or dens. He gradually wound his way up through the granite and pegmatite crystalized chasm with its looming peaks and dizzying cliff walls on each side. White water cascaded below at times over vertical chutes but the main floor of the canyon rose slowly most of the time. The wind had switched and was coming out of the west here. The strong katabatic breeze slowed his progress, but he finally emerged on the westward side of the mountain range and dropped into another grove of pines. He slung his hammock and woke when daylight began to tint the clear sky to the west. He slung his pack and slowly rose from the floor of the canyon. It was a very calm morning even at an altitude around timberline, and the tops of the peaks off to his right were beginning to get the sun's first rays at a breathtaking height. Cin guessed four of the peaks surpassed twice timberline.

At first the valley ahead seemed about like any other, but he became curious, and after he descended a couple thousand feet and magnified his vision he could tell this was not the case. There was steam rising from the floor in dozens of places, maybe even hundreds. The whole gargantuan valley lay in a geothermal caldera like noting he'd ever heard about in any scroll from any generation. No one had ever been there or it would have been documented. As he dropped lower he could see that some of the flora and fauna were very unique, and he guessed he was farther south than he'd predicted. The short palms were growing in small groves around the ponds and

springs along with other species of slender drooping ferns. The mountain towering to the north of
the valley appeared to be volcanic but it hadn't been
active for eons, and some of the snowy peaks in the
smaller range to his south were also coned or pyra-
midal caused by molten fissures.

He circled down and absent mindedly checked
his windage before dropping to the ground beside
the large slow moving river. The gravel bank was
about thirty feet wide and tapered out where the
stream made a bend to the west. The grass was three
feet tall where rock met rich dark volcanic earth.
There were outcroppings of mixed forest, and many
huge grassy clearings and swampy areas. The river
wasn't brackish looking but he decided to replenish
his water supply from a fresher stream nearer the
mountains anyway.

Cin stood in the center of the valley and gazed
at the strange panorama. The sunrise was turning
the mountains to the north a bright pink now and
he could see several sivilin at about timberline gliding far in the distance nearer the tallest peak. He
walked along the stream for a few minutes checking for tracks but was disappointed. All he came
across in a quarter mile was a moolarine trail leading through the tall grass from the river to a grove of
saplings where the animals had been cutting small
trees for a dam in a branching tributary.

He just caught the tail end of a striped reptile that appeared to be about two feet long as it disappeared into the foliage, and this new discovery made him very wary. Land dwelling reptiles called kluim were known to exist in the Moktaw islands; sometimes the creatures could reach twenty feet in length and they were carnivorous.

The snow at this latitude dropped to about timberline on the side of the mountains all around him, and the rainforest in the valley was overgrown with ferns or foliage and grasses almost six feet tall in places. It was a paradise for sivilin. The giant flying scourge could probably live indefinitely on the vegetation here with no animal proteins in their diet at all.

Cin realized that in all of his life he'd seldom been in such a picturesque place, and he also realized that he'd never been so filthy. He'd been traveling for weeks without a decent bath. There was a hot spring running into the tributary near the moolarine dam, and after he quickly searched the area for kluim or other dangerous predators that might be lurking in the undergrowth he took a dip in the stream and washed his lightweight leather clothing. He even washed his hammock while keeping a close scrutiny for danger either on the ground or in the air.

He saw sivilin as they entered the valley in groups, but they were always flying alongside the mountains, perhaps for the thermals and ridge lift the radical terrain provided. He counted nine in one bunch and six in another. He failed to sight any kluim or other reptiles on the ground but he could hear strange unfamiliar sounds in the night and was awakened at times.

Cin spent a few days in the scenic valley and enjoyed the hot spring while snacking on pine nuts, palm nuts, and delicious wild fruits that were different than any he'd ever seen to the west of the Desowan wilderness. He also enjoyed several different types of ripened berries that were abundant and grew in some of the various hot or cool springs and pools. He topped off his unusual diet with a flying moolara that he killed with his crossbow. His arrow broke at the tip when it went through the animal and he only had four remaining in his quiver so he checked the area for some good straight shafts the next day.

He had a few obsidian arrowpoints, some sinew strands, and extra sadegaudi feathers in his pack. All he needed was tree sap from a manta sapling and he would be able to make a few arrows. There was a grove of mantra willows near a muskeg about a half mile from his camp, so that morning he set to work. It was a nice sunny day, not rare weather it seemed for this warm climate; though it did seem to rain almost every day. The grass near the muskeg was as tall as his chin but he packed a trail into the willows alongside the swamp while watching for slithering vermin and found five good shafts. He flew back to his camp after scraping some valuable sap from a few mantras and by mid-afternoon he had three more arrows that met his satisfaction.

The almost complete absence of animal life in the sterile rock and ice of the arctic he'd just transgressed had been depressing and boring. He was glad to see colorful songbirds in the valley of the sivilin, and realized that he would never take their friendly presence for granted again.

Leaving the valley that night wasn't as easy as hiding in the seclusion of the pine grove amidst dozens, perhaps hundreds of sivilin, but as was the case in the Desowan, the gigantic flying reptiles seemed to always den up at night. He flew westward slowly after the sun set and watched the silver moon rise an hour later. The red moon had already risen.

With his nocturnal vision he was able to see very clearly with almost no cloud cover, and after scanning the sky he was fairly sure he was safe. Cin searched the wave rifts for a neural signal after he reached timberline, but there was nothing. He hadn't sensed even the slightest of stirrings since crossing the polar ice.

All of the klute colonies would be celebrating in a few days. There would be feasts and music and wines and brandies in all of the colonies for several days celebrating the week of the zinda hunter. The full moons only appeared in the sky beside each other once every year, and a complete eclipse every five years was celebrated with a huge gathering by all of the klute colonies in the glacial cirque at Sagitar. A close proximity of the crescent moons also occurred late in the winter, and the event was celebrated with a night of image sharing and beverages and a feast of sorts. Sometimes games of skill were held at the ceremonies mostly involving weapons and targets. Some of the other games involved image sharing and game pieces or even small tanned numbered skins.

A low lying range of mountains spanned the western horizon and he encountered an eastward flow of air as he neared them. There were no glaciers here but the tops of the peaks were completely snow covered. He flew through a pass between two rounded mountains at about timberline and noticed that the sky in the west was already getting lighter. To his surprise there was a marine layer of fog on the far side of the mountains. The fog bank was a good distance below, but stretched for as far as he could see toward the west. The light headwind slowed him here slightly, but he continued his journey undaunted.

Cin flew west for most of the morning and the sun was high in the sky when he saw water below a broken ceiling of cloud that was at about a quarter timberline. He wondered if he was over another sea or perhaps just a large lake. Cin had to quell his anxiety when emotions of solitude and danger became almost overwhelming again.

CHAPTER SEVEN

Arak, Shandra, and Enneka leveled off near the steep talus slopes on the western side of Mount Sagitar and banked downstream above the river just to avoid scrutiny by the elders or any other bystanders that might be concerned about youngsters or students attacking sivilin. Arak led the way and they touched down by the river about a half mile from the village.

"Well that was definitely another terrifying experience." Shandra looked at Arak and then pulled her quiver around to check her supply of arrows. "I think we'd better make a lot more of the quad bladed arrows and make sure all of the sivilin hunters try them."

Arak nodded. "I hope no one was down there with the chalows. I hope everyone is ok."

Enneka's moccasins made loud scrunching sounds on the gravel riverbank as he walked toward them.

"Those arrows are amazing." He said matter of factly. "Wish mine had been a little lower, but I think I might have it in the eye or something. They fly so straight in the wind. You guys hit it right in the throat again." He laughed off his apprehension and the other two joined him as was usually the case after a near death or at least a very dangerous experience. "Maybe we should try for more eye shots." Enneka projected an image of his arrow's flight and it actually appeared to hit the sivilin in the head near its left eye.

"I'm just glad to be standing here alive right now." Said Shandra. "Besides it would have to turn its head sideways or something." She began laying her arrows on the smooth rounded stones of the gravel bed. "I think I'm going to throw all of my old shafts away and make new double bladed ones this week. The quad blades don't veer off at all in the wind."

"I have seven of them." Said Arak. "I'll give you each two of mine and we can make some more. I think we are going to get busy. The sickness is spreading to the upper terraces and caves now, and it seems to linger for days and days. My mom is feeling a little better but I think it's been almost a week since she got the fever."

Shandra looked up from where she was kneeling taking a drink of water. "My young nephew is almost better, but my mom and dad are really sick. Seems like age plays a factor."

Most of the students are fine." Replied Enneka. "They just get the sniffles for a few days, but the grown ups are really getting sick, and some of the elders are even dying. I felt like I was getting it a couple days ago, then it just went away".

"Me too." Arak slung his quiver and checked the wind. "We should fix up one of the old lookout towers on top of Mount Sagitar or Thunder and keep watch during the day."

"Good idea." Shandra looked up at the gigantic peak. "We can work on our weapons up there if we can make a wind break."

"Let's go up and check it out then." Enneka slung his quiver and they all lifted off heading downstream into a light wind.

There was no sign of the wounded sivilin. It had disappeared over the mountains toward the Desowan.

The old abandoned lookout tower on top of Mount Sagitar was in a disarray. Rocks of all sizes and angular shapes were laying around scattered by the wind, rain, and ice over the decades or perhaps centuries. The tower hadn't been used for a few generations, but most of the materials were still there. The hurricane force winds that often battered the summit had blown all of the snow away, but there was icy frozen snow below them all of the way around the mountain. The three young klutes began stacking stones carefully around the small depression that had originally been the floor of the structure.

The wind picked up a little on top as the day progressed. The mountain sloped off very steeply on the east side and was windswept and rocky. It was about the same on the west but there was deep frozen snow and ice for a quarter mile before a sheer cliff dropped off for about two thousand feet. There were more gradual inclines to the north and south, and they were also covered with ice. They worked all morning and had one side of the old structure stacked about four feet high with a wide layer of rock to block the wind from the east. The prevailing winds were usually from the east, but oftentimes the western fronts would tear at the upper reaches also.

The shelter was about fifteen feet long on each side. Enough room for a few sivilin hunters to rest and watch in comfort. Shandra worked on arrows all afternoon while Arak and Enneka stacked rock. Making a couple small windows was the hardest part, but after some of Magahila's long forgotten cliff dwelling crafting lessons kicked in they were successful.

The sun was getting low in the east, and suddenly lightning did a dance across a dark sky to the north of Thunder mountain stabbing at the lower peaks beyond. They decided they'd done enough work on the shelter.

They snacked on stuff they had in their packs while watching the sky. It was a nice enough day with very little wind, but at the altitude of timberline and a half it was cold. They would bring zinda furs up and make a collapsible roof out of chura hides in case of sleet, snow, fog or mist, and stack more rock in their spare time. Mount Sagitar made the best lookout vantage with its elevation above the surrounding peaks. Sometimes it would be above the clouds while the rest of the mountains were shrouded.

The three young klutes disembarked the mountaintop when it was just about dinner time in the big cavern. They decided to find Duroon after checking on their families. They would see if he needed help with anything. It seemed that all of the middle aged and elder klutes were suffering from nausea, fevers, or respiratory tract infections. Most were not able to send or receive even the simplest of images after acquiring the high fever that seemed to go along with the virus.

The disease had spread like wild fire throughout the whole Sagitarian colony in the past couple of days. Out of almost five hundred klutes at least four hundred were down with the sickness, and many others were very weak while recovering from the severe fever. Most of the students were busy helping Duroon care for and feed the ill. The rest were busy gathering wood and fresh vegetables or medicinal plants for soups that were easy for the sickly to digest. The Sagitarian colony was completely defenseless.

Arak and Shandra walked up the stone staircase and entered the main cavern just as a light rain began to fall. A sudden flash of lightning lit the white bleached Sivilin skulls that lined the entrance giving the place a deathly ghostly omnipresence.

Duroon glanced up from the foremost cooking fire. "Where have you two been? Your mother was wondering if you were ok. Said something about you guys hunting up north. We had a terrible occurrence here today. A sivilin came right to the ground and killed one of the chalow herders. Her name was Sory. I don't know if any of you knew her. She had impaired wings and has been unable to fly for many years."

Arak knew who she was but wasn't acquainted with her. Enneka and Shandra said the same thing and they were all alarmed and sorrowful. Sory had a daughter in one of the younger classes of the academy.

"Not much wild game around." Arak sat on a big chair near the fire about twenty yards from the huge cave mouth and gazed out toward Thunder mountain for a moment; then he focused his attention on the dozens of sick that were laying around. Most of the woodpiles that were usually kept at waist level within the cavern were only about a foot or two tall.

"Looks like the wood supply is getting low." He said.

Duroon glanced up from his work. "I have some students bringing it, but they are kind of slow. I hope they all get back here before the lightning gets too bad. I'm glad your mother is feeling a little better today. She ate some mikta steak for the first time in almost a week. Shandra's parents are sick. They seem to be taking turns caring for each other even though they are both ill. The virus definitely weakens at times but then it comes back. All we can do is try to keep everyone's strength up and hope imaging skills will return when the fevers subside."

Arak placed a piece of wood on the fire and sat back down. It felt good to rest after stacking stones all day. "My mother had some cakes for breakfast too, but she looks pale and still has trouble breathing sometimes. She won't come down here. Her fever isn't that high and she wants to stay at home. She says she can take care of herself so I guess as long as somebody goes by there a couple times a day she will be fine. I wonder why you aren't getting it?"

Duroon picked up a container and glanced at him. "I've been one of the caretakers for the ill for so long that it probably has already run its course through my veins, but I do get kind of weak at times. I feel like I'm coming down with it for a day or so and then my body seems to fight it off. I've had a cold and a runny nose for a week now but it never gets any worse. I can still see images, but not from out of line of sight. What makes me curious is why the younger generation seems to be immune. Usually it works the other way around."

"Rhee and Dulles both have it. Not all of the students are immune, in fact I think most of them have the sniffles and some have slight fevers." Duroon sat across from Arak and frowned at Shandra who stood near a small nearby table. "Most of them are losing imaging skills too."

Duroon poured warm sadagaudi broth from a clay pot into a bowl. "Dulles was passing blood like some of the others but he seemed a lot better last night. I guess we will have a death ceremony for Sory tomorrow night. Her family and especially her daughter is very distressed."

He extended his wings and stretched while wiping mucus from his nose with a thin shammy. He looked tired and glum when he took the bowl to one of the more sickly patients laying in a hammock a few yards from the side wall. He glanced back. "We are lucky enough to have a few hunters around that can still defend the city from a sivilin attack. We can't have them wandering around in the colony. No one likes piecing together the bodies after sivilin attacks. Someone dove on that one today but I'm not sure who. They must still be out over the Desowan."

Arak and Shandra glanced at each other for a moment. Arak was glad Duroon hadn't tried to pry into their memories as he had in the past at times. It was considered rude and an invasion of privacy but sometimes the younger klutes at the academy were subject to mind probes if it was deemed they were hiding something causing them to miss their lessons.

Duroon strode back toward the fire and began stocking another cooking pot with vegetables, herbs, and skinned shredded sadagaudi breasts. "Savant took a turn for the worse yesterday, but he's tough. He keeps making himself eat the broths we are making to ease the pain. Allie is with him up above and Magahila is in her dwelling above also. They are almost incapacitated, but Allie is strong enough to link with my mind at times if I'm in her room, and she can stand and move around like Miz. We are bunching the ill together so they're not so hard to care for. The elders are all worried about students out hunting and gathering with no supervision. You guys better stay close to the city from now on until we get this under control. Magahila doesn't want any of the youngsters straying far unless they are gathering wood up north, but I think Nooney has some of them checking the chalow herd."

"We can stay around and help out if you want." Arak glanced up from the cooking fire's hypnotic flames for a moment.

Duroon produced a rare smile and looked at Arak and Shandra almost as if he was hiding a feeling of admiration. He scratched his short grey beard. "We will be needing extra wood so if you want to go up north to the aspen groves tomorrow and help the others go ahead. Just keep a lookout for sivilin. In fact it might be a good idea for someone to stand watch somewhere along the mountain front."

Arak took a thick shafted arrow from his quiver and held it out for Duroon to examine. The older klute looked at the point and handed it back. "They break too easily." He shrugged. "I tried a couple on miktas and the points are too weak where you file through the shaft. They can't be used again like the single blades."

"I've; well we've." Arak motioned toward Shandra. "We've been practicing with them and they are much more accurate in the wind, and we put up a wall on

Sagitar where that old look out shelter used to be. We can sit out of the wind up there now if you want someone to stand watch."

Duroon looked at the arrow in Arak's hand and laughed. "Well if you want to spend twice as much time as you need making arrows nobody is stopping you I guess. The ancients used them for some reason; or at least made some of them, but I think it was more for ceremonial purposes. Our ancestors used to worship the moons you know, and leave offerings for good luck. Some of our generation still do. Don't let Magahila or any of the elders know you are practicing with weapons without supervision. I know they are all sick, but they can still give orders. They'll have you cleaning the latrine or serving lunch and looking after the youngers in the academy for a couple weeks. If you want to stand watch up on top of Sagitar for awhile every day that's fine. Just get down here as quickly as possible if you see any sivilin."

Arak wished his father was there and quelled emotions of anxiety for his missing parent. Cin would know what to do. He would be able to project images to his father and show him the amazing accuracy of the quad bladed arrows without getting in trouble. As far as religion was concerned Arak thought that it was irrelevant. When he was very young he'd asked his father what happened to the dead after they were gone. Cin had pointed at the tanned Zinda fur on

Arak's bed. He'd simply stated. "The zinda doesn't worry about whether there's an afterlife. Why should we."

Arak watched Duroon mix his soups and herbal teas for a minute and wondered if Orem had said something about them diving on the sivilin of which they'd shared the images. Orem was also very sick, and remained in the lower anteroom of the main cavern in his temporary dwelling with his mate Shilo who was also ill.

Duroon looked up from his work for a moment. "I forgot to tell you. I think Magahila wanted to see some of you from the graduating class. When you see Enneka tell him will you? She has some projects or chores for you three. I forgot to tell you yesterday. If she doesn't have anything important for you to do you can fly up to the top of Sagitar for awhile I guess. She probably just wants firewood."

Arak didn't mind gathering wood, it was quite a distance to the sapling groves, and wood was heavy, but a definite chore that couldn't be ignored.

They left Duroon and walked up the narrow carved stairway to Magahila's dwelling in the upper caverns along the western side of the entrance to the main cave. The huge sivilin skulls loomed just to their right as Arak ducked beneath the awning and entered the doorway. A friend was sitting in a hanging chair swinging slightly while making something with an awl and twisted chura hair that had been made into thread. It was gloomy in the room but three candles glowed on the table.

Her name was Roopa and she was about Magahila's age but unable to fly due to her weight and partially crippled wings. The big female klute stood as they entered and put her tools aside. Her wings were small and shriveled from no use, and her face was chubby. She was clad in dark colored leather, and her stomach stuck out over the belt holding up her pants. She walked over toward a fireplace alcove that had a smoke hole leading to the outer cavern, and picked up a plate. It was stacked with lystocakes and she held it out for Arak and Shandra.

Roopa spoke with a nasal voice. "Magahila wanted to see you, but she's asleep now. She said if I could find you, Shandra, or Enneka that I should tell you to stay close to the city; don't be going far from the colony looking for easy hunting. She wanted me to have you help Nooney look after the younger classes in the academy until her or Orem recovers from this plague."

"No problem." Shandra took a bite of cake. "We can watch over them and keep them busy I guess."

Arak knew the big female had been born with very little use of her wings, and he felt sorry for her whenever he saw her. There were others like her but usually they couldn't fly because of injuries or nerve damage. There were also illnesses of sorts. Sometimes a brain fever of some kind could even make it hard for them to walk for many years after it passed.

Arak stood next to the doorway of Magahila's dwelling and took a cake from the plate. He was peering down at the floor of the main cavern. Lightning flashed again and thunder rumbled. The ill were laying around below, and there were more in the catacombs of cliff dwellings along the sides and back walls of the cave. There were dozens of bed-ridden klutes throughout the large shelter; most on hangings but many were resting on sleeping pads on the floor.

Some of the younger classmates from the academy flew in through the huge doorway of the main cave and landed with packs laced with wood. It was almost dark as they began stacking it near half a dozen fires that were burning. The roof of the huge main chamber was high and slanted up enough that smoke simply rose out of the entrance to the east most of the time. Very seldom did the wind blow straight in causing any problems with the air on the floor or even in the anterior of the huge shelter.

That night Arak ate with Miz. They discussed trivial matters and why Cin had been gone for so long. They were worried about him, but Arak was just glad she was able to eat some solid food and breathe without the rasping sound she'd been making at night.

He retired to his anteroom in the upper cave and crawled beneath the tanned zinda furs on a soft moss and grass packed mattress made of sewn skins. He held the ceremonial arrow for a moment and turned it over before blowing out the candles and laying it on the night table beside his raised bed. There was also a hanging or hammock by the doorway, but Arak preferred the wide bed when at home. Sometimes Shandra would stay with him, but she was with her parents tonight.

The dreams started slowly at first; just random flying dreams; mostly swooping and diving along the rims below Thunder mountain. They went on and on with no apparent direction or meaning, then suddenly a sivilin's black and red streaked horned face came up over the rim. The huge thing opened its mouth baring two and three foot long fangs and shrieked before clamping onto one of his legs. Arak woke with a start; his heart beating almost its maximum rate. He wasn't hot but he was sweating profusely. Klutes rarely sweated but the dream had been so horrifying that it took him a few moments to calm himself.

He got up and went into the main room and saw his mother sleeping soundly. Cool water was in a clay vase by the door, and he poured himself a mug before going back to bed. He wondered if he'd eaten something that caused the nightmare, then shrugged it off and went back to bed. He realized that he'd handled the artifact before going to sleep, but to think that it was causing some kind of images or dreams was just ridiculous.

The dreams came again, but this time they weren't so shocking and he slept on. Arak was flying above one of the monsters at a good altitude, maybe timberline or higher. The sivilin was at about three quarters timberline and unaware of his presence. Arak carefully moved himself into a position behind the thing out of its vision and began dropping very silently toward the creature. His crossbow was loaded when he pulled in right behind the sivilin and slightly above. He aimed carefully and pulled the trigger sending a thick shafted serrated quad bladed arrow toward the reptile's head right at the base of the back of its skull. Arak didn't wait to see if the arrow found its mark. He opened his wings bringing himself to an abrupt stop, then dove past the sivilin's tail. The huge creature shrieked and twisted its whole body in a spasm as it tried to claw at the missile lodged in the back of its head, and it seemed like it was half paralyzed for a moment before it started spiraling toward a wasteland made of eroded towering buttes high mesas and crevasses filled with thorny kishka thickets.

In his dreams Arak swooped behind a massive mesa in the Desowan. He was looking for some place to hide when he finally woke again. This time he was sweating slightly again, but his heart wasn't racing. He dozed off again and slept soundly for the rest of the night. He'd had nightmares about sivilin even before he'd helped his friends attack them.

Arak, Shandra, and Enneka went to the schooling cavern the next morning and tried to organize the younger classes. The elders that usually helped the instructors and made up their projects and lessons were all sick. Only one of them remained. The klute that was in charge of the place was almost like Roopa and just barely able to fly or glide. Her name was Noony and she was very frustrated walking around with a willow switch threatening to use the harmless weapon on some of the misbehaving students. The whole academy was in a complete disarray. Some of the younger students that were not able to fly yet were having some kind of a food fight at one table and another older class was laughing gleefully while instigating the pandemonium. Only a few of them even seemed to be the least bit worried about the current disaster that was afflicting the whole colony or the sivilin that had killed a chalow herder right in their midst.

Nooney was overweight, she had light auburn hair and blue eyes. Her wings looked normal, but they were stiff from little use. A simple spotted taral fur tunic hung from her shoulders and she wore short leather pants like many of the females in the summertime. A big jade pendant hung impressively from her neck and rested just above her breasts. It portrayed a carving of a sivilin, and not a bad representation in the world of klute artwork. Leather strapped laced moccasins were wrapped in a criss crossed pattern around her thick legs upward from her ankles to her knees.

She got everyone's attention and decided that the only way to keep order would be to have an election so each class could have a leader of sorts. This was fun for the students and they agreed with anticipation. After each class had a leader or supreme, they selected one more from each of the age groups that could help the leader oversee whatever projects they were doing. Everyone settled down and the willow switch was retired to the woodpile in the kitchen.

Noony decided that many of woodpiles were low after discarding her switch, and told Arak to have at least ten from the older classes fly to the sapling groves beneath the rim of Thunder mountain. The thin bark on hundreds of the younger saplings in this area had been ringed at the bottom to kill them, and the dry wood was easy to harvest in four foot lengths after notching part way with obsidian axes and breaking with stones. The older students were all prolific with the ax. It was one of the first chores they were given as soon as they could fly with a loaded pack.

Of Arak's graduating class only five out of eleven were able to perform chores due to the plague that was infesting itself in Sagitar. Yas and Saran were both in the schooling cavern, and they met with Arak, Shandra, and Enneka. They discussed the day's plans while eating a big breakfast that they helped prepare in the kitchen, then they set about their tasks. Fifteen of the younger klutes went with Yas, Enneka, and Saran to the sapling groves while Nooney, Arak, and Shandra organized the other classes with their elected leaders that were still present.

The weather was calm and sunny so as soon as everyone was busy Arak and Shandra left Nooney who complimented them and said she was grateful for their help. They took off for the lookout shelter on top of the mountain. The sun had been shining into the canyon for about an hour already, and thermals were rising nicely. They circled upward in a nice column of warm air along the front of Mount Sagitar and soon they were above timberline. No sivilin could be seen; just some mawls were soaring above the pass between Thunder and Sagitar looking for small furred prey that lived in the rocks and boulders at the higher elevations.

The klutes were almost hovering in the wind as they neared the shelter on top of Sagitar, and they touched down lightly. They admired their handiwork. The shelter looked kind of small, but it would suffice. They'd stacked a lot of rock and the eastern wall was almost as high as Arak's shoulders. They'd also made a row of stones to establish a base all around the indentation that had once been the floor of the lookout post.

The two of them began stacking stones and Arak realized that his hands were sore from the previous day. His muscles were also stiff and sore, but after working for awhile he loosened up. Shandra wrapped his blisters with a piece of soft woven cloth that she'd brought for flint or obsidian knapping, and he continued working on the lookout tower for a couple of hours. He reinforced the eastern wall tapering it in toward the top while leaving a small window.

The sivilin was almost over the divide before Arak saw it, and he quickly shrugged into his qiuiver and slung his crossbow as he warned Shandra. The thing was coming up out of the Desowan toward the northern pass. It was almost impossible to see against the background of the wasteland, but Arak had been diligent while he worked and he'd detected movement about two miles to the east. They huddled together in the shelter and watched through one of the ports that they'd made in the wall. They watched and waited patiently for the sivilin to fly through the gigantic swale between Thunder and Sagitar. The wind was coming out of the east today, and it was a good ridge soaring breeze. A swifter flying sivilin would be able to overtake them if they were discovered and couldn't get out over the canyon far enough to drop at a safe speed so they simply hid within the shelter.

Arak could feel Shandra's breath on his face as they peered through the small window, and he could tell she was breathing faster than normal. The sivilin flew upward between Thunder and Mount Sagitar about a hundred feet above the barren rocky saddle. It was traveling at a good speed with the tailwind, but the two young klutes still waited a while before taking flight.

They flew swiftly after leaving the shelter, and rose upward with strong ridge lift just off of the eastern face of Mount Sagitar. When they were a few hundred feet above the pass they let the wind take them west out over the canyon.

Shandra picked up the sivilin with her keen vision as soon as they were over the canyon. It was circling down toward the colony. This was the second or third one in just a few days that was curious enough to search the lower canyon for wild game, and when it could see the couple dozen speckled brown, or black and white chalows grazing on the plateau just above the klute city it made a change in course.

"No one is watching the chalows so lets do like we did the other day." Arak swiviled his head and looked at Shandra. "Let's wait till it is coming up with a chalow and put some arrows into its neck if we can. We can drop into the thick forest below the tree houses if it follows us."

She tried to grin, but he could tell she was very anxious as was the case whenever they dove on one of the creatures.

"I'll be right beside you." She said with conviction in her voice. Arak could tell she was scared, perhaps terrified of the sivilin. He guessed he was too, but if they were careful they should be able to escape the claws and teeth of the monster as they had in their previous encounters. They both had quad bladed arrows in the grooves of their bows as they drifted out over the huge abyss to the west of Mount Sagitar.

The steppes on the other side of the canyon were the main focus of the sivilin as it dropped toward the chalow herd. Arak squinted and magnified his vision and could see the creature's splotchy light green and brown camouflaged skin as it plummeted toward the brush and grassy meadows above the klute colony. The long plateau to the west of the canyon rose many thousands of feet before slanting to the west into the Moon Creek drainage. Some simply called it the Moon Creek divide and others sometimes referred to it as the Froze to Death plateau.

The sivilin landed on the slope in the midst of the chalow herd and had one in its talons before the small goatlike animals even knew they were in danger. It ripped the chalow open with its teeth and began to feed nonchalantly. It was in no hurry, and after a couple of bites it had completely consumed the entrails. It lifted off sweeping gigantic wings. It lumbered downhill on slender legs at a fairly good speed; its tail switched back and forth a few times as it became airborne. Soon it was drifting out over Froze to Death creek and the Sagitarian colony. It rose slowly with the remains of the chalow in its talons and when it was out over the eastern sloping foothills of Mount Sagitar it seemed to catch a warmer column of air and it began circling upward still using its wings.

Arak and Shandra had drifted slightly north and as they soared the upper reaches above the pass between Thunder and Sagitar the sivilin slowly flew up out of the canyon. When it was at about timberline Arak let the wind take him out over the creature. Shandra was right beside him when they dropped from about fifteen thousand feet to attack. They fell as silently as possible and the sivilin was unaware of their presence until they fell headfirst in front of it. The creature threw up its head in the usual surprised manner and the crossbow bolts flew. Both bolts struck the thing in the throat within a couple feet of each other and the sivilin let out an angry terrifying shriek that could be heard clearly for perhaps a mile or more.

The two klutes plummeted headfirst wings folded tightly and the sivilin banked to follow. It was about a half mile behind as they neared three quarters timberline or twenty five hundred feet above the ground, and Arak adjusted his fall slightly as he sent Shandra an image of the forest below. They weren't very far from one of their early childhood camping spots.

They had made some treehouses and had learned to camp out in the forest after they'd passed certain flying and ridge soaring tests at a young age. He was aiming for a clearing on the side of a steep hill that lay north of the colony's secondary hot spring. He could see steam rising from the spring as it flowed into the river off to his right. Arak spread his wings slightly to slow his fall. The sivilin was safely behind, still shrieking at times in an angry frenzy. Arak glanced upward and could see it directly above him as it spiraled toward the floor of the valley. It was clawing at its neck trying to remove the crossbow shafts now, and it seemed to be losing its interest in the klutes.

He looked to the side and could see Shandra not far from him as he spread his wings and flared for a landing at the edge of a familiar thick deciduous forested patch. He'd gathered firewood here when he was five or six years old and could barely fly with a pack.

Shandra landed next to him and they ran up a narrow game trail beneath the leaf covered canopy of branches. The air in the forest was pungent with its smells of decaying leaves from the fall before. Grasses, flora and fauna were sprouting up through the thick layer, and he could see some nice leafy legumes off to his left that would help to spice up a stew someday, but he could hear the sivilin coming down into the clearing already. As it touched down it let out an ear shattering scream that reverberated through the trees.

It was terrifying enough to send Arak and Shandra into the air and they flew up the path swiftly where it was wide enough dodging branches as well as they could. When they were beneath the pines and mixed forest they angled toward an old childhood project. The treehouses were just ahead and Arak picked one that he'd help construct when he'd been learning how to fly ten or so years before. Shandra knew where he was going and they reached the tall coniferous trees a minute later running and sometimes flying through and between the giant branches. They flew up into the crude shelter that lay about fifty feet up the side of the tree. They both stood on the floor and looked at each other for a moment listening for the sivilin. Arak could see that the floor had been recently tied in place with new hemp lines by a younger class from the academy. Two big branches supported the structure.

The sivilin was well behind but they could finally hear it coming through the trees breaking and snapping branches with its massive body and wings. When it was within the thickest of the pines the two klutes took flight again and struggled up through an opening just big enough for them in the upper canopy of branches. They were soon above the forest and on their way north toward the cliffs along the base of Thunder mountain where they would hopefully catch a thermal. The sivilin was safely trapped beneath the branches and would either have to topple a few trees somehow, or exit the forest before it would be able to take flight and follow them. The ploy worked exactly as it was supposed to and Arak was glad they had learned the tactic from Orem a few years before.

"Hurry!" He looked back a Shandra. "Let's get to timberline again!"

"I'm doing the best I can!" She was using her wings frantically trying to keep up with Arak.

Even when they were very small he'd been slightly faster than her, and that was not always the case with klute gender. Oftentimes females were faster than the males due to their more slender stature and smaller musculature. Except for Yas; Arak was usually the fastest flier in the graduating class, but most of the students were very competitive.

There was a thermal rising from the bare rocky boulder strewn floor of the valley near the towering crevassed monoliths of Thunder and they quickly circled upward. The two of them were at three quarters timberline or twenty five hundred feet above the ground before the sivilin wandered out of the forest. It came out on the same side that it had entered. The winged creature shook its head and clawed at the crossbow bolts again before clamping its claws around the remains of the chalow. The sivilin's fifty foot wings beat the air and it lifted off propelling itself forward and upward at an amazing speed for such a large animal.

Arak and Shandra continued spiraling upward in the strong thermal. There were puffy broken clouds above the rising column of warm air at a little above timberline. They hovered beneath while the sivilin rose up and began a slow ascent in their general direction. The dead chalow was hanging limply from the claws of a hind foot. The two klutes were north of the main pass, and that was what the sivilin appeared to be heading for.

The flying nemesis had its meal for later in the evening and was heading back out toward the Desowan where it would lair up. The hot dry air of the wasteland was where the sivilin seemed to prefer spending most of their time. They could soar and thermal much easier on columns of hot air rising from barren rocky canyons, and crumbled mesa tops. Big fat slow moving horat were usually plentiful along with the long grasses around kishka thickets, and there were literally thousands of caves of all sizes and even huge underground chambers for them to reside in where they could hatch their eggs without danger from predators. The tops of the mesas were usually studded with small twisted gnarly pine trees known to the klutes as Picaru bushes and the long grasses also flourished amongst them during the summer months. Most of the wider canyons were also usually grass filled at the lower elevations even in winter; except where flashfloods washed down from time to time burying everything with a soft claylike mud.

Shandra hovered beside Arak circling very slowly as they watched it come. "What are we going to do? It's coming fast. If it sees us it will attack."

He looked away from the sivilin for a glance in her direction. "Let's dive on it again."

"What?" She was startled and dumfounded. He could tell she wanted to just go hide in the patchy broken cloud ceiling that was manifesting itself over the valley.

"Why not." He said matter-of-factly as he adjusted his quiver and pulled the thin leather covering away from the feathered shafts. He quickly handed one to Shandra. It was a quad bladed arrow. He removed another one from the quiver and replaced the covering so he would be able to drop at terminal velocity without any wind resistance from the quiver.

The two klutes drifted toward Mount Sagitar and rose up into a little cloud on another thermal. They were invisible now but the air was bumpy in the cloud so they rose up and out above the mist using their wings. The sivilin was unaware that it was being stalked as it pushed toward the pass.

They attacked it on the west side of the divide and again the sivilin threw up its head as if surprised. Both crossbow bolts hit it in the neck. It banked as if to follow again, and when Arak and Shandra plummeted downward toward the Sagitarian river it began clawing at its throat.

They were both looking up between their laced moccasins at the creature as they plummeted head-first with arms and bows tucked tightly against their torsos. They were at about timberline when the thing shook its head violently and shrieked in frustration.

To the klute's delight and relief it leveled off and left the chase: the dead chalow was still dangling from the claws of a hind foot. It soared upward on a thermal and disappeared over the pass just after Arak and Shandra slowed their descent about a thousand feet above the ground. Arak had failed to noticed on the first skirmish that the giant flying lizard was completely missing the tip of its right wing, and it also had a long tear in the left wing.

They hadn't been very far from some of the wood stockpiles below Thunder mountain when the sivilin had chased them into the forest so they landed near one and began gathering kindling. Enneka, Yas, and Saran suddenly appeared overhead and Arak pointed in their direction. He could even hear them speaking as they flew.

"We have friends." He said.

The other three landed and it was obvious that they hadn't seen Arak or Shandra's battle with the sivilin.

"We thought we heard a sivilin awhile ago." Said Enneka as he touched down. "Did you see anything?"

Arak knelt and tied a knot on top of his pack that would secure a long leather line for ferrying wood. Enneka was walking toward him and Arak looked up.

"We had another sivilin encounter this morning." Said Arak with a frown. "Thing came down onto the steppes below the divide and got a chalow. We had to hide in the trees below here."

Yas was very excited and Arak could tell she was a little bit afraid. Her sandy colored hair was cropped almost as short as his and she carried a crossbow and quiver along with her wood laden pack. "How close to the colony did it come?" She asked. "Was anyone hurt?"

Shandra was also tying knots for a line to hold wood on her pack and she answered for Arak without looking up.

"It took a chalow from the Moon Creek divide."

They sat on granite moraine and ate lunch in the sunlight, then Arak and Shandra began loading their packs with dead wood that they'd gathered. Mostly dry driftwood from along the river bank. It was nice to have some kindling around the fires, and the other three had heavy loads of cordwood that had been chopped and broken with axes. Duroon would be happy to see five loads of wood.

Shandra sat down and shrugged into her heavy pack after sitting it on a big flat rock.

Saran was helping her adjust the straps between her wings so the sticks wouldn't hinder her flying. A little striped rock sprite was chattering and scolding them from a jumbled pile of stones behind them. It was a perfect sunny summer day for those who weren't sick with plague. Or ripped to sherds by a sivilin.

Yas was still worried. "What if the sivilin is still in the canyon?" She asked.

"It went over the pass just before we saw you." Arak glanced at her and could see that she had a concerned look on her face. He put his pack on the same rock as Shandra and shrugged into the straps. They all hoisted their loads and after a slow jog into a light breeze they lifted off and flew downriver.

Duroon was glad to see that they were all ok. He said he wasn't sure, but he'd thought he heard a sivilin shrieking somewhere. By the time he'd gone outside for a look it was gone. He pointed to different stacks of wood that were getting low.

The sick lay all around. Some were standing and walking from time to time but most were too weak and just sat or slept in hammocks, chairs, or on soft matts. Breathing was usually a problem so many slept or rested while sitting or being propped up in their hammocks. There were only seven in the main cavern able to move around like Duroon, and two of them were slightly ill, hacking and coughing. No one seemed to be getting much better, but most were able to eat small portions. The students were sad to hear that there had been another death that morning. One of the elders had passed away. Her name was Feresy and she had been in perfect health before the sickness. Duroon and the others had done everything in their power to save her, even trying to cool her fever with glacier ice at times.

Arak deposited his wood quickly, took a small pot from Duroon, and flew up to his small family's alcove across the canyon. Miz was glad to see him back, but still too sick to fly.

"How is Duroon doing? He hasn't been up here today." She asked as Arak pulled the awning shut to keep out the breeze. He lit a big fat candle that had wax rivulets sticking to the sides, then stirred the fire in the hearth before adding kindling. He could tell someone had been there or the hearth would have been completely cold.

"He's still healthy." Answered Arak. "We just brought him some wood. He said he will be up to visit later."

"He's amazing. I worry about him all of the time. Almost as much as I worry about your father. I thought I heard a sivilin. Did another one attack the colony?" She raised herself up and leaned back against a rolled zinda fur in her hammock. She coughed almost uncontrollably for about five seconds.

"Yes." Arak put a pot of stew that Duroon had given him over the tiny fire that was starting to thread its fingers up through the dry sticks. "It killed a chalow and flew up over Thunder pass into the Desowan."

She frowned. "I hope one of them doesn't try to go into the main cavern. We are defenseless. There will be more coming into the canyon now with no sivilin hunters over the Desowan."

"All of the students and everyone that can shoot will put crossbow bolts into its face." Said Arak. "I don't' think we have much to worry about. If one tries to get anybody it will meet at least twenty crossbow bolts. Shandra, Enneka, and I have been fixing up the old lookout tower on top of Sagitar. Someone can watch from there from now on. Duroon thinks it's a good idea. I think some of us might go back up there this afternoon and work on it a little more."

Miz coughed again for a moment, then stood and walked to the doorway. Her breath was short and she was kind of wheezing but Arak could tell she was a little better today. She looked down at the valley floor and the chalow pens. The colony had about fifty of the small goatlike animals and a couple would not be missed. She'd known Sory personally though.

"I think it's a good idea to fix up the old lookout towers." She said. "There's one on Thunder too, and another one on the divide way down by the lake. If you see sivilin just get down into the forest as quickly as you can or come right to the main cave."

Arak nodded. He wouldn't worry his mother about their recent activities in the air. Miz tried some of Duroon's stew and Arak bid her farewell.

He dropped from the small cave and met Shandra at the academy. Enneka came along and they soared back up to the lookout post after helping Nooney organize a late lunch for the students at the school. It was about six miles to the top from the colony.

The afternoon thermals were strong, and soon they were soaring a column above timberline that took them up below a cloud at about fifteen thousand feet or timberline and a half. The top of Sagitar was just off to the east and they dropped toward the lookout tower or shelter. The wind was coming out of the west today, and they let it take them over the top then they flared and touched down easily near the ancient rock structure. The wind was light and variable sometimes gusting to twenty miles an hour, but that was nothing at their current elevation. Usually the wind was blowing at least thirty or forty miles an hour coming up over the snow streaked divide. It was cold, and Arak pulled a light jacket out of his pack. He shrugged into it and quickly tied the thick leather laces holding it in place around his wings so they would be free as he entered the shaded doorway of the structure. He was happy with the work they'd done and Enneka commented on the progress that had been made since his last visit.

Arak found a thin flat rock that he'd been using as a scoop and began removing sand and dirt from the floor of the shelter so the walls would be a little higher. It was just soft dry sand and stones that had fallen inside when the structure had toppled. Enneka took the stones outside and stacked them while Shandra worked on arrows. He was able to lower the floor almost a foot along the north wall, and was scooping along the west side when something shiny caught his attention.

Arak laughed out loud and held up a perfect arrowhead. He'd quit worrying about the recent turn of events for the time being.

"Hey! Here's one you won't have to make." He handed the obsidian arrowhead to Shandra and she laughed along with him. Enneka looked at it before he took a big stone from Arak.

"Wonder how long that has been there?" He frowned. "Looks like an old one."

Arak kept digging and scooping out the dry blown sand, and a minute later he removed another large flat stone. He looked down after he handed it to Enneka and saw something that made his heart race. It was a slender piece of the black, timeless, Desowan greasewood. A very old piece. He carefully brushed away the dry sand around the thick decrepit shaft before removing it. The arrow was still intact and the huge ancient obsidian arrowheads were still in the grooves where someone had placed them eons ago. The artifact was just like the one Arak's grandfather had given him. He held it up and showed the other two, and they were all speechless for a moment.

The dense heavy greasewood was crumbling around the outside, but most of it was intact, and it still held the obsidian arrowhead. The aperture in the end was cracked and wide open on one side but the hooked serrated knife blade was still in place. The klutes used the greasewood mostly for chairs and tables within the caves when they could find big enough bushes. It was virtually indestructible and would not decay for eons if it was kept fairly dry. It was hard to find, but grew within and around some of the kishka thickets in the Desowan.

"The wood is so amazing." Said Shandra. "Orem said some of the tables in the main cave are over five hundred years old; older than the most of the archives."

Arak turned it over. "The one my grandfather gave me is in better shape, but just the same design. Whoever made this knew how to kill sivilin."

He handed the arrow to Shandra and she replied. "It's amazing that something so old could survive up here for so long. The knife shard is a little longer than the ones I'm making, but I can make them exactly like this."

Enneka spoke up. "Maybe whoever used this one had a bow with a stronger pull."

Shandra handed it off to Enneka, and he examined it.

"Maybe." Arak looked at him. "The greasewood is heavier than the willows we are using too." The climate on top of the mountain is dry. I think the wind keeps the place bare all year round. The top of Sagitar is usually above the cloud ceiling. That's probably why the wood is still intact."

Enneka handed it back to Shandra and she hefted it again. "It is noticeably thicker than our old shafts, and you're right about the rain and snow. If we find a body up here it will surely be mummified." She laughed as the breeze ruffled the long guard hairs of her hooded jacket. The inside of the hood was made of wolflike mada fur and she had it tied under her chin. She offered the arrow back to Arak.

Arak just waved his hand and laughed. "You can have it if you want."

"You found it." She insisted. "Besides what am I going to do with it. You should keep them together."

Arak glanced back into the shelter. There was almost always a cold wind on top of Sagitar, but they were all using hyperoxygenated blood at the high elevation and Arak didn't really feel it. All of them were wearing jackets, long leather trousers, and lined moccasins.

"Maybe we can find some more old stuff in there. I found some broken pottery the other day." He put the arrow carefully under the flap of his quiver that was leaning against the stone wall. "Are you sure your mother wouldn't like it? She likes old antique stuff."

"No. You keep it." She said with conviction in her voice. "Keep them together."

The three of them worked on the shelter for a couple more hours and decided they better go help Nooney with the school children. Most of the very young had been moved to the main cave and were being looked after in a couple of the cliff dwellings by Duroon and his skeleton crew, but there were still trouble makers in the academy's two big classrooms. Nooney was unable to control a few of them for some reason.

They held a brief ceremony for Sory that evening and everyone that could attend tried to console her daughter. A cousin of Sory's was one of the few that could still fly and do activities, and with a friend accompanying him they'd taken the remains to the burial site south of the city.

After the ceremony Arak and Shandra went to the big hot spring up the trail behind the main cavern. A shelter had been partially constructed over one of the warm pools, and there were scented oils and soaps on a rack. They enjoyed each other's company sexually, and afterward they oiled dry spots on each other's wings with scented oils that had been made in the Baden river colony.

Shandra's parents were still sick but her mother was getting over it slowly. Her father was covered with blisters and still having problems breathing. They continued staying in their alcove next to Miz's, and Duroon or someone from the main cavern would make rounds a few times each day checking on everyone.

Enneka's parents were also both in their high alcove in the cliff above the school. They were in about the same shape as Miz. The pneumonia kept coming back weakening them whenever they exerted themselves very much. They were able to move about their small alcove and do menial tasks by themselves, and they took turns boiling teas and broths.

Arak, Shandra, and Enneka scanned the sky carefully before dropping off of the mountain, but they could see no sivilin. Just a group of dark feathered mawls soaring a thermal way below them over the edge of Thunder pass. They all went to their homes, then after checking ill family members they met with Nooney at the schooling cavern. Duroon was there and he was happy with the way they were doing things. He said that electing class leaders had been a brilliant idea, and he was glad they were fixing up the old lookout post, but he said he wanted more firewood.

The three of them helped Nooney that evening at the academy, then they spent the night with their sick parents. Arak slept a little better, and Miz seemed to be getting over her cough. Shandra said she slept well also, but Enneka looked rough and said his mother and father had been up for most of the night again.

They flew up to the sapling groves after breakfast, and after they deposited a load of wood Duroon decided they could go up and check for sivilin at the lookout shelter. They looked in on their sick families before catching a strong morning thermal that took them all of the way to the summit. They scanned the skies for sivilin but all they saw were the mawls soaring over the same spot off the side of Thunder pass.

"Hmm." Enneka gazed out over the vast expanse that compromised the western edge of the Desowan wasteland. "There's something dead over there or that many birds wouldn't be circling in the same thermal."

Arak nodded. "I think so too."

Shandra was removing her pack and getting ready to make arrowheads, but she suddenly stopped and Arak helped her secure it back between her wings.

"let's go." He said, and they launched into a strong breeze coming in off of the wasteland.

The sivilin was huge. It lay on the bare slope about a thousand feet below the pass and fifteen or twenty mawls were feasting on the dead behemoth. They could barely stand the stench as they landed and walked up to the crumpled body. One of the gigantic wings was outspread and the other was beneath the torso. Its head was bent back at a strange angle and its neck appeared to be broken. The tip of the extended right wing was missing.

Arak walked up to it and pulled one of the crossbow bolts from the creature's neck. There were four of them embedded in its upper neck and throat, and he carefully cut them out with his obsidian knife. One appeared to have hit the jugular vein or main artery going to the creature's head; either that or it had clawed at the shafts causing one of them to tear the artery. The grass was blood stained all around the thing's front legs and there were dried pools beneath its chest. Arak held up one of the arrows and showed the other two a quad bladed point.

They had killed their first sivilin. It was the one that had taken the chalow, and Arak and Shandra's persistence in attacking it twice had paid off. What was left of the chalow was actually laying down the slope a few hundred yards from them, and was also being consumed by mawls and other scavengers at an alarming rate.

"They are even bigger than I thought." Shandra squeezed her nose to keep out the stink and her voice sounded funny. She stood near one of its front claws and looked at the dead creature. It was a large one, and probably had a wingspan of a hundred and ten feet. Four or five dark feathered Mawls were hopping around on its calico colored back greedy for the free carrion that had been provided for them.

The creatures had evolved over the eons to blend in with their surroundings like the rest of life on the planet. They walked clear around the dead sivilin examining its features especially taking note of the huge claws and teeth. None of them had seen one up close yet; just in image sharings. The marbled blotched browns and greens on the creature's back melded in with blues, greens, and light greys mottling the underside. It was beautiful in a way, but deadly; and completely wiping out chura and mikta herds at an alarming rate in the Desowan and along the mountains to the north of Sagitar.

"You two will be pretty famous at the next image sharing." Enneka walked along the steep grassy slope so the wind was taking the foul stink away from him.

"Don't tell anybody but Orem, or maybe Duroon." Shandra looked at him. She still had her nose pinched and her voice was nasal. "And you better not tell him until some sivilin hunters are able to fly again." They all sat down on the rocky slope and gazed upon the dead creature in awe.

"I wonder how many there are?" Enneka gazed out over the Desowan again. "Orem says there's never been a record of so many invading the delta in any of the archives."

The wasteland looked barren and sterile, but they knew there was abundant animal and plant life in the nooks and crannies of the arid landscape below.

"Someday let's go down in there along the bottom of that first big canyon that runs to the south and look for some greasewood to make arrows." Said Arak absentmindedly.

"What did you do with the one you dug up yesterday?" Asked Shandra.

"I gave it to my mother." Arak looked at her and frowned. "She said it might be a bad omen, but I think she is just worried. My father has been gone for over three months."

The wind was picking up slightly, and they soared with the mawls for a moment before reaching altitude and gliding back toward the lookout post. The three of them tinkered around for most of the afternoon sort of taking turns scanning the sky. There were no sivilin, and they were happy with the crude old structure that they'd reassembled. It kept out the wind and all three of them could sit inside comfortably and work on their weapons.

That evening they helped Nooney again and were glad that two of the most ill in the main cavern were showing signs of recovery. Someone else besides Duroon had been with Nooney that afternoon also. One of the fifth grader's mothers was getting well enough to fly a bit, and she had helped with the night chores.

Arak and Enneka dreaded helping at the school, and Shandra let them go home early after they'd finished dinner. She stayed and helped Nooney with a few menial chores.

Arak took a bath in the hot springs and was glad to find that his mother was able to sit up and do some crafting of her own. Miz was working by firelight coming from their brightest lamp. A small pot filled with chura tallow. She was stitching a thin pair of lightweight fur leggings or trousers when he entered the alcove. They visited for a few minutes and then Arak went to his room and lay down. He put the two ancient arrows on the headrest of his bed and snuffed out two thick candles. He had a strange feeling that maybe everything was going to be all right in the colony and he dozed off.

The broken dreams came slowly and intermittently; then they began to coalesce into deep rem sleep. He slipped farther and farther down into the recesses of his subconscious mind and the nightmares became vivid. He woke up about midnight with a start and found that he was sweating lightly just like the previous time when he'd had the dreams. They weren't as vivid as the first time and he went into the living room where his mother was sleeping. He drank a glass of chalow milk, and noticed that most of the ice was melted in their small cellar. He returned to his room and picked up the two arrows. He examined them in the darkness; comparing them vaguely before he went back to sleep.

The dreams came again with a vengeance. Vivid dreams causing the unconscious mind to drift into a state of complete reality. Arak was flying above a sivilin. He didn't dive on the creature in the preferred method of attack. He stalked it silently from behind and above slowly dropping into bow range. When he was no more than thirty yards from the sivilin's head and about even with its tail he carefully aimed his crossbow. He flew up between the monster's huge sweeping wings and pulled the trigger.

The images in the dream or the vision itself were out of Arak's control, and he had no choice but to await the outcome. He rolled over on his back in the air reversing direction as swiftly as possible and dove past the sivilin's tail just missing it by a few feet. He didn't see where the arrow went but it had been streaking toward the back of the sivilin's skull when he'd made his dive. The thing didn't follow him or try to rake him with its talons this time. It appeared to stiffen up like a zinda that was stretching in the morning sunlight after it had just come out its den. The sivilin's body simply went limp after the initial death convulsion and began falling toward the Desowan.

Arak followed the dying sivilin for a moment before waking up and realizing where he really was. He got up and walked to the doorway of the main alcove. He pulled the awning aside and looked out at the bright moonlit night. It would be a good night for travel. Both moons were full and almost coinciding. He wondered again if the ancient arrows were sending him images somehow and decided that he would be foolish to think so. He realized how tired he really was, and after checking to see how his mother was breathing he went back to his room.

Arak moved the two timeless artifacts to a table in the corner of his room. Moonlight shining in through the small port through the outer wall cast a faint glow on them. He realized that the colony was missing one of its favorite holidays. The double full moon fest usually brought klutes to Sagitar from all corners of the delta.

He slept soundly for the rest of the night and awakened remarkably refreshed. Arak tried to remember exact images of the nightmares, but was unsuccessful. He would have shared them with Shandra or Enneka but for some reason he was unable to focus on them or retrieve them from his memories well enough. He could just remember fragments or depictions of the strange nightmares that had been racing around in his mind. It was a rare trait for a klute to share dreams, but not impossible.

Arak had one memory of the recurring dream that seemed to be imprinted. He was almost between the wings of the sivilin and aiming at the back of the creature's head with his crossbow. That image was etched in his mind and would be there forever. The rest of the dream was just a jumble of puzzled blurry images.

They did their morning chores, hauled a load of wood each and then had to help move all of the younger children back to the anteroom of the academy. Three of them had come down with bad colds, and Duroon decided to move the rest away from the sick adults in the main cavern. A few more adults were able to get around now and they would be able to help Nooney look after the youngsters. There were only eleven adults able to walk for any length of time, and four able to fly short distances. None of them were sivilin hunters. The rest were completely incapacitated; flat on their backs or sitting up so they could expel the viral phlegm from their lungs. It was a devastating sickness in several ways.

After lunch Arak, Enneka, and Shandra flew back up to the lookout tower and worked on weapons. There were no sivilin, but a supercell thunderstorm was manifesting itself over the Desowan and moving slowly westward. They decided to get down off of the mountain before the lightning became a threat.

CHAPTER EIGHT

Cin gazed and squinted, magnifying his vision. He searched in every direction for a land mass, but was disappointed. All he could see was water. He decided to drop below the broken cloud base for a better look. When he was over a wide opening in the cloud ceiling he descended about five hundred feet. He was still a couple thousand feet above the ocean or lake and could see for thirty or forty miles. He was relieved beyond words to finally see a white line in the distance. Waves were breaking on rocks or a shoreline along the western horizon.

He was able to spend the night in a deciduous forest in his hanging, and there was no rain. The forest was full of furry moolara of several species, and he killed and cooked one over a rotisserie the next morning.

Living off of the land was easy as he continued westward hopping thermals and using the prevailing upper flow of air, but he was disappointed to find no landmarks of any kind that had been mapped by the klute race. Only one mountain peak manifested itself, and he'd never seen it on a map or in a scroll. It was to the south and rose perhaps quite a bit above timberline because the circumference of the upper reaches of the pointy volcanic peak was snow streaked.

The going was very slow even with the upper flow of air and long days in his favor. Lightning storms were frequent, especially during the hot humid afternoons when rising thermals were at their peak, and they would pound the lands with rain and even hail. Sometimes the storms would rage from early afternoon into the early hours of the following morning.

He was curious about the absence of sivilin, but the area was heavily forested with very little fern overgrowth or lush grass that would offer forage for the creatures. They didn't seem to like eating leafy materials like one of the smaller mikta species. There were very few open parks or clearings, just trees from horizon to horizon. There were lots of miktas however. He spotted them from time to time and even heard some zinda growling one night while they were feeding on something.

On some days he would only be able to fly for three of four hours before lightning became a threat. The summer was way beyond solstice when he met his first sivilin since crossing the last open channel or sea. The creature came from above timberline and through a break in the clouds surprising him. It almost got him in its clutches. The talons nicked him and slashed through the outer skin or dactylopatatigum medius of his right wing for about eight inches, but the bones remained intact. Cin was able to plummet seven or eight thousand feet and elude the creature in the trees.

Luckily klute wings regenerated and healed very rapidly. He would stay and let it heal completely so he wouldn't lose any of his future maneuverability. He was able to find food easily in the southern forested area while it healed. The lands were teeming with wildlife. Moolara were plentiful and he killed one with his crossbow the first day while just hunting on foot. The arrow went through the small animal and sank deeply into the bark of the tree trunk behind. He was able to dig it out and save it with his dagger.

Cin tried to sneak up on some miktas the next morning but the deer were much to shy and wary. They disappeared into underbrush as soon as they heard him crunching on leaves or twigs. He surprised a taral the same morning. The two foot tall spotted cat was feeding on a moolara that it had just killed. He left it alone and laughed as it carried the large moolara off perhaps to a den of half grown kittens.

Cin wasn't an expert at setting snares, but the second day he spent in the thick deciduous forest he tried making some moolara snares to save on arrows. There were plenty of phiranuts scattered around on the ground beneath a species of giant leafy phiratrees, and he found a relative of the Sagitarian terravine fruit hanging from some of the short trees along a stream. He broke open the thick shells of the phiranuts with granite stones.

He speared a few small fish that afternoon and decided to make a temporary campsite near a bend in the stream where there was a good fishing hole about four feet deep. There were no materials around for making good weapons, but all he needed was a carefully crafted long triple pronged sharpened stick to get fish.

He'd been flying slowly northwest and seemed to be out of the palm forests, but there were tall ferns and another type of reptile that he wasn't familiar with. He saw a few of the creatures but they were only about a foot or two long and seemed harmless. They were colorful bright greens or light blues with yellow or orange stripes running the full length of their slender bodies. He seemed to remember seeing an image of the creatures at a sharing but it was a long time ago. He doubted if they were poisonous.

He heard zinda calling out a few times and sometimes the nearby lizards would cause a resounding din throughout the forest just after dark in order to establish territories or mating rituals. There were always mawls squawking at daybreak and other various birds would join in the chorus. Cin had hung his hammock from two thick branches about ten feet above the forest floor in a phiratree after carefully climbing lower branches with his damaged wing. There was no way to stitch the cut to help it heal, but it would mend on its own in a week or so anyway.

He was sure he was getting close to mapped and explored land. If he kept flying northwest he would eventually see some landmarks or come to one of the large slow moving rivers that lay to the east of the Desowan wasteland. There were vast plains and rolling hills to the east of the Desowan, and he guessed he was no more than two or three days from the grasslands or one of the main drainages. He hoped he wouldn't encounter more sivilin and decided to try to find a higher stream of air to take him the rest of his journey home. He would have perhaps the most interesting or sought after images to share for at least a generation. He had crossed the arctic sea and had somehow come back over the polar ice and down the east coast. He would just take his time and make sure the images could be shared for future use and exploring by the klute race.

Cin used ferns and some long branches to make a canopy over his hammock and keep out most of the rain, and he was able to make fire in the damp forest if he dried grass and moss in the sun for a few hours. He covered coals with a flat rock in a deep recess between two tree roots when he was foraging, and was able to keep a fire going for several days at a time.

He cooked fish and one morning he killed a small horat with his crossbow. Cin had just awakened from his night's sleep and the animals were rooting and snorting around beneath his tree shelter. The fortunate turn of events were a welcome respite from his sneaking and creeping around in the forest, and after he made a tripod rotisserie for cooking he enjoyed one of the best meals he could remember since crossing the tundra and northern Serlian mountains.

While his wing healed he just explored the nearby forest and its bounty of fruits and nuts. He realized that he'd never seen so many moolara. The small animals were darting from tree to tree staying just out of his sight most of the time. There were black, grey, and even rust colored moolara. The rust colored species could all fly or glide from tree to tree on a thin layer of skin with outspread limbs.

He worked on his shelter and weapons. Zinda were around. He saw tracks and heard them squalling and fighting from time to time after darkness, but they paid him no mind. He hung the cooked horat in a tree about a hundred yards from his shelter and carried scraps and unused pieces of the carcass far downstream. He dried and smoked some of the horat meat and still had some left over twelve days later. By then his wing was healed enough to start flying again.

Thunderstorms were still frequent, but not quite as severe as he'd encountered to the southeast. It was hot and humid and pesky insects were almost intolerable about dusk. he would be glad to get back to the delta and the cooler climate of Sagitar. He ground up a mixture of stinky swilgrass and stimroot to repel them from his skin every night, and kept a fire going for awhile each evening with wet moss and leaves placed on top. This made a nice smoke smudge at dusk and drove most of the insects away.

He resumed his journey homeward early the morning the fourteenth day after being attacked by the sivilin.

CHAPTER NINE

Arak stood in front of the lookout shelter and looked out over the Desowan. He pulled the hood of his lightweight oilskin jacket back and noticed Shandra was doing the same. The sun was just coming up behind them and high cirrus clouds were starting to lose their brilliant orange colors. It was a cold morning on the mountain as always, but there wasn't much of a breeze for a change. Enneka had decided to stay with his ill parents for the day and just do some chores for Duroon. He'd said he wasn't feeling so well himself and didn't feel like flying up to the top of Sagitar.

Shandra suddenly pointed to the left of Thunder mountain; her breath was visible in the cold thin air. "Sivilin." She exclaimed. "I see at least three of them."

Arak saw them immediately even though they were a couple miles away, and he nodded. "Looks like they're going to come over the north cliffs into the delta."

Duroon had given the three students from the graduating class permission to hunt in the early morning hours, but he didn't' know they were dropping in front of sivilin. He assumed they would be hunting one of the chura or mikta species that used to thrive on the delta.

"Should we try to put some arrows into one of them?" She asked.

"The forest below the cliffs is pretty safe." He looked at her and frowned. If anything happened to her he would feel terrible, but she was a perfect shot and they'd eluded the flying nemesis several times with no problem.

"Let's see if we can get high enough. There won't be any thermals yet but we are already above them here at launch." He loaded his crossbow, extended his wings, and jogged down the slope a few steps before taking flight. Shandra followed him and they banked out over the canyon gaining altitude as fast as they could. There was just a slight breeze coming in along the pass between Sagitar and Thunder mountain, and they used it to their advantage gaining several hundred feet in just a few minutes as they flew northward.

Arak turned slightly east to avoid being seen by the sivilin, and they continued climbing as they soared out over the rocky abyss that dropped from the mountain pass in jagged terraced intervals for almost three vertical miles. The sivilin were about a half mile below them and completely unaware of the klute presence. Arak and Shandra were using hyperoxygenated blood at about eighteen thousand feet when they banked to the left and followed the three sivilin back over the northern edge of Thunder mountain.

They could see no reason to wait, and they wanted to lure the sivilin away from Sagitar anyway so they attacked as soon as they were out over the canyon far enough to get down into the safety of the trees if there was a chase. They decided to dive on the one to the right, then take a trajectory toward the forest below the cliffs along Thunder where the trees were the tallest and thickest.

The two young klutes from the Sagitarian academy dove side by side as silently as they could. The sivilin were flying in a slight vee formation, and when Arak and Shandra were about a hundred yards above them the one on the left sensed something and looked up.

It was too late, and by the time it let out a loud shriek and banked for an intercept Arak and Shandra were dropping in front of the sivilin on the right. It seemed like slow motion maneuver for Arak. He wished he could fall faster and get a more accurate shot. He wanted to be as far from the terrifying creatures as he could as soon as possible. He aimed carefully, allowed for fall line drift, knew the creature would raise its head and pulled the trigger. Quad bladed arrows flew and the klutes plummeted headfirst as fast as they could in the usual manner.

The wind at terminal velocity made verbal communication impossible but Arak looked over at Shandra and saw that she was smiling. He realized that he was grinning back and gave her a positive hand signal with his fist clenched and thumb raised. Both arrows had hit their mark. The black streaked faces of the sivilin could be seen above as they followed. The one that had sensed them first was only about two hundred yards behind. The two klutes were outdistancing them rapidly, and by the time they were below three quarters timberline they were able to alter their course toward the cliff wall where they'd practiced shooting targets.

They were still twenty five hundred feet above dense mixed forest where some of the pines and leafy deciduous trees were over a hundred and fifty feet tall. The upper canopy of branches in this area was ideal for eluding sivilin.

Arak glanced back a couple of times before they flared out of their dive and began slowing for a landing. He doubted if the sivilin would come all of the way down. They'd been so high when they'd loosed their arrows that they were over a half mile ahead of the three creatures. He absent mindedly followed Shandra as she turned and swooped into the trees. They were out of sight now but they would keep moving.

Luring one sivilin into the forest and escaping had been easy, but he didn't know what three of the menacing monsters would do if they decided to hunt as a pack. He doubted if they would work together to kill prey however. Duroon said they weren't equipped with that kind of wolf or mada pack mentality. They ran and flew through the trees toward the north and up over a small rise. When they were a quarter mile from their entrance into the forest they chose a big pine and rested on branches about a hundred feet up. The three sivilin never came close to them but Arak spotted movement through the branches above. He caught a glimpse of the three monsters as they flew overhead a few thousand feet above them. One of them was lagging back and seemed distressed and he hoped the arrows had injured it.

"At least we got them to follow us away from the colony." He said.

"Shandra looked down at him. She was sitting on a branch just above and slightly behind. She sent him an image. "My arrow hit right next to yours. I hope it claws at them and rips out its own throat."

He could feel the slight tingling and closed his eyes even though he'd seen her arrow hit the sivilin right after he'd fired his own. She'd been able to shoot perfectly and the arrow had hit a fraction of a second after his. They were both buried almost to the feathers in the animal's soft neck about a foot from each other.

"What did you bring for snacks?" He asked.

"Mikta jerky, and some terravine is all." She answered. "Want some?"

"I guess so. Sure." He stood on his branch so he was even with her and laughed. "Sivilin hunting makes me really hungry for some reason."

"Yeah, me too. And the altitude on top of Sagitar makes me famished all the time just like flying in the high thin air." She turned around so he could reach in her knapsack. "It's under the top flap."

They waited about an hour before leaving the forest and scanned the sky very carefully before taking flight. The three sivilin were nowhere to be seen so they flew along the base of Thunder mountain where the hot summer sun was already doing its work. There was a nice thermal with a couple of mawls soaring above the rocky canyon floor so the two klutes used it to circle and soar back up about five thousand feet to timberline where a small cloud was starting to form. They left the thermal and flew south along the mountain front, then used ridge lift until they were over the pass. They searched the skies carefully as always but saw no more sivilin. A few minutes later they were at the lookout post.

The two of them had stashed some lightweight furniture and materials for making arrows in the structure. They began the slow process of making more serrated knife edged quad bladed arrows. Practice helped and they were getting faster at making them. By noon they had each completed an arrow and had begun grooving out the center of another for the dozen or so knife blades that Shandra had painstakingly made over the past week.

They took a noon lunch break and sat out of the wind on the east side of the shelter. It was warm for the altitude but they still wore their thin oilskin jackets.

"Duroon is going to get suspicious pretty soon." Said Shandra as she opened her knapsack and began looking for something to eat. She found a package of lystocakes and handed one to Arak.

Arak handed her a flask that contained water. "I know. We will just have to do the best we can until there are some sivilin hunters that can take our place."

She took a drink and handed it back while suppressing a cough. "I've been fighting this cough for a couple of days. We probably shouldn't drink out of the same flask."

We're not carrying two water jugs all the way up here, or anywhere." He laughed. "If we get sick we can stay at my mom's place. I think I'm getting a cold too. I've had a sore throat for a couple nights now, and I'm having trouble receiving images from anyone; just blurry stuff."

Arak suddenly stood up after he finished his snack and looked back out over the canyon. He sensed someone coming. Shandra had felt the tingling also and she closed her eyes.

"I think it's Yas." She said. "But I'm not sure. I can never tell her presence in the rifts from Tillery or Saran, and my imaging skills are being compromised too."

Arak walked around the lookout structure and shaded his eyes. He could see someone now and he magnified his vision. It was Saran and she touched down lightly, almost hovering with her sleek wings in a ten mile an hour southeast wind. She had an oilskin jacket and slacks like the others and her dark hair was cropped at the shoulders.

She smiled behind dark intelligent eyes and looked around. "Enneka told me what you have been doing up here. Have you seen any sivilin?"

Arak and Shandra both laughed and Shandra pointed toward Thunder mountain. "We saw three of them this morning." She said. "They went up north and crossed the canyon by the cliffs before we lost sight of them."

"Enneka is feeling sick this morning." Saran looked in the shelter. "Wow. You guys really fixed this up. You even have chairs and a table."

"My mom had an extra wicker table and chairs." Arak strode past her and entered the shelter. Three chairs and a small table dominated the center of the room where they'd been working on their arrows. There were a couple of unfinished products laying on the table and Saran picked one of them up.

"What is this thing?" She asked simply. "Why all the blades?"

"We are making a few arrows like my old ceremonial artifact." Arak picked up the other one and checked the feathers to see if the glue holding the sinew was dry.

"Oh." Saran put the arrow down and peered out of the small window. "This must keep the wind out pretty well. My mom and dad said it can blow so hard up here that it's impossible to fly sometimes.

They said to be careful whenever there are lenticular clouds up here."

They visited about the sickness and chores that needed to be done. Arak said he didn't think they would run out of firewood with all of the students pitching in now. The students were neglecting their studies, but they could catch up. There was still plenty of meat stored in the ice caves and anyone that was very sick could not eat much anyway so hunting wasn't a priority. The Sagitarian river was also very good trout fishing but klutes almost always preferred red meat to fish or seafood.

They were glad to have a friend for company, and later that afternoon they decided to go look for a horat. They departed the lookout tower and quickly dropped two vertical miles before starting out over the tiered partly forested foothills above the Desowan canyons. Saran had never been into or over the Desowan, but she knew Arak, Enneka, and Shandra had been out there many times. Enneka and Saran were becoming close friends. He'd confided in her but she still didn't know they were trying to shoot sivilin with their crossbows.

It took three klutes to carry all of the meat of a decent sized horat, and they killed one in a thorny khiska thicket about half an hour after reaching a briar patch drainage that dropped into the first main canyon of the Desowan. They set to work and soon they had the meat stripped and packed.

They were just starting their flight up the east slope when something caught Arak's eye. There was a cluster of greasewood bushes growing near a spring that flowed out of a niche in the nearby granite cliff wall. He swooped down, removed his pack quickly, and began looking for his obsidian saw. It took him a minute to carefully cut a few branches that weren't warped or curved too much. He decided they would be good enough to be used for arrows with a little straightening, and they resumed their journey back up the mountainside. The wind was picking up a little and they finally circled and soared a nice thermal.

Some of the ill were mending slightly, but they were still unable to fly due to the extent of the pneumonia like symptoms. Any exertion at all seemed to cause their fevers to come back. Orem was so sick he could hardly speak so Arak and Shandra visited him and Shilo in their high cliff dwelling that evening. They hoped he would recover but it was very depressing for them to see the leader of the Glass Canyon colony so meek and helpless. Shilo was able to move around and perform light tasks but still unable to fly, and she was covered from head to toe with blisters and pimples.

Savant was able to walk around for awhile each day, and according to Duroon he could cough and hack loud enough inside the main cavern to wake anyone within shouting distance. Many of the ill had pimple like symptoms all over their bodies, and some even had them in their throats making it hard to eat, drink, or even speak without a horrible rasping.

Arak and Shandra were feeling better the next morning and after spending the night with Miz they flew down to the main cavern. Duroon was looking through scrolls and had several spread out on a table.

"How is everyone doing?" Asked Shandra.

He glanced up and smiled when the two youngsters approached. "No one else has passed away for three days now, and some of the worst are losing their blisters." He said. "We might get through this after all."

Shandra looked at the writing on one of the scrolls. It was several hundred years old. "What are you looking for?" She queried.

"I've been going through these old things looking for a similar incident. This one is from four hundred years ago." He answered as he held up a rolled piece of dry faded tanned mikta skin. It was so old that it could hardly be opened without having pieces crumble off the sides.

"I can't find anything that has decimated any of the colonies this bad. Just some flus that caused some deaths, but they always passed within a few weeks. This sickness has gone rampant all through the delta. Visitors from Taro and even a few from Sagitar have been to the islands recently. It seems to have started there."

Students were arriving from the schooling caverns; crowding around waiting for instructions pertaining to their daily tasks. Duroon started organizing them and getting groups going off in different directions. Arak and Shandra said they were going hunting and he just nodded.

It was cold and a brisk wind was coming in from the Desowan when they landed beside the lookout post. They went inside immediately after a quick scan across the eastern sky, and Arak began working on some new shafts. It wasn't very cold when they were inside out of the wind even with no roof, but the structure had very thick walls at the base and they tapered as they rose so they deflected most of the rushing air straight up.

The clouds were getting thicker and thicker to the west and by midmorning they could see nothing below them in that direction but a sea of clouds. Tempest and Froze to Death mountain looked like a couple of small islands with their pointy granite tops just poking through the clouds. The rest of the nearby peaks were all shrouded. It was still mostly clear over the Desowan however, and the wind had died down somewhat.

No sivilin approached that day, and they were able to make a few more arrows. They wanted to stockpile as many quad bladed crossbow bolts as they could. Later in the afternoon they had to contact Duroon and get a directional singularity so they could drop through the layer of fog. The signal was very dim, but they managed to link even with their hindered skills due to the virus. They broke through the thick ceiling about five thousand feet above the colony and circled down into the overcast canyon.

That evening there was news that some students gathering firewood up near Thunder mountain had found a dead sivilin. Supposedly it lay about two miles west of the river toward the northeast side of Froze to Death mountain. The monstrous creature had a deep gash in its throat and had apparently bled to death. No one could figure out why it was wounded unless it had been perhaps fighting with another sivilin. The students hadn't done a closeup examination of the carcass for very long due to the stench.

Arak and Shandra found the dead sivilin the next morning and were able to retrieve part of one of their crossbow bolts. The creature had clawed and torn the other one out of its neck, and the serrated razor sharp obsidian quad blades had sliced through its jugular vein in the process. Shandra's prophecy of having it cut its own throat had actually come true.

"Huh." Arak stood motionless for a moment and looked at the dead sivilin in awe. It was formidable looking with all of its armament showing even though it lay dead in a huge crumpled pile. Mawls were squawking and jumping around on its back. One wing was outstretched and the other lay back beside the carcass. "We got another one."

Shandra wiped her forehead and just remained speechless for a minute while examining the broken arrow he'd handed her. "I remember making this one."

The sun was still below the western rim, but it was tinting the upper cliffs and granite ramparts of Thunder mountain a faint rose color as it climbed higher. The wind was beginning to sigh through the pines.

"Now we know why the ancients made quad bladed arrows." Arak laughed.

"We're going to need more." She answered. "But we still better not tell anybody what we're doing or Duroon will ground us."

"I know." He frowned. He knew the rules of the academy would apply and be taken into account foremost no matter what kind of disaster was striking the colony.

It was sunny that morning with just a few wispy cirrus clouds. The clouds were probably at almost three times timberline and were made of ice crystals. It was very calm on top of Sagitar making it a rare day. Two sivilin came in from the Desowan about mid-morning but they turned and flew north along the east side of the range so the klutes left them alone. It would have been hard to catch up with the flying nemesis anyway.

Saran joined them about noon and had a nice surprise for them when she opened her pack and handed them lystocakes soaked and glazed with honey. They were all sitting around the west side of the shelter soaking up the sunlight when a dark ominous shadow suddenly crossed the divide right in front of them. It was another sivilin. A loner this time. It was barely three hundred feet above the mountain when it shot past and began banking un-steadily toward the north in bumpy air caused by ris-ing thermals along the western mountain front. It was looking down into the canyon as if curious.

As soon as Arak thought they were out of danger he motioned for silence and ran into the shelter for his pack and weapons. Shandra and Saran followed, and they hastily armed themselves and tied their knapsacks tightly at their waists. They'd lost sight of the sivilin for the moment but when they were out over the canyon Shandra's keen eyes spotted it right away.

"What are you going to do?" asked Saran. "It's starting to circle. It's going to go down into the canyon."

Arak turned his head and looked at her. He didn't see anything on her clothing, or quiver that might make noise at a high speed.

"Can you dive without making a bunch of noise?" He asked.

She checked her belt and made sure nothing was loose that might rattle or make strange sounds in the wind. She had a small tote tied at her waist instead of a knapsack, and she secured it tightly so it wouldn't move.

"Sure." She answered. "But you aren't really thinking of diving on it are you?"

Shandra was standing down the ridge a few yards shading her eyes while scanning the sky. She answered for him while laughing.

"We dive on them and try to keep them away from the colony."

Arak and Shandra already had arrows in their bows, but Saran's was empty and she only had a couple of arrows in her quiver. She'd never been a very good shot when falling along the cliff wall shooting at the targets but Duroon had complimented her and said she was showing the most improvement.

"Just follow us and stay off to the left of Shandra. Don't fall too fast. Just try to stay even with us. We fall at about the same speed as when we are shooting the targets. We will try to put a couple of arrows into its neck. We'll dive toward the forest below the treehouses after we shoot."

"I can try too." Saran reached back and lifted the flap on her quiver. "I brought some arrows, but I think we will be severely punished for sivilin hunting. I don't mind taking care of the impaired, but I hate washing dishes and cleaning the bathroom."

"We've done it before with no problem, and who's going to punish us? They're all dying or something." Arak smiled and tried to reassure her. "Just wait until you are slightly below it and aim way high. At least six or seven feet. The sivilin will probably raise its head and your arrow will be falling as fast as you just like when we shoot at the targets. If we can time it right we'll be about the same distance from the sivilin as we are when we fall along the cliff during practice."

Shandra spotted the sivilin as soon as they were out over the canyon and she pointed. Arak saw the huge flying lizard about two thousand feet below and a mile or so north. He adjusted his flight slightly so they would have an intercept position. The sivilin was circling slowly down into the canyon losing altitude gradually. It was making wide oblong circles and Arak thought it looked like an ideal set up.

They were at about seven thousand feet when they made the intercept. Arak fell on the right; Shandra was in the middle, and Saran was on the left. It seemed like slow motion for Arak again as he plummeted down in front of the creature's black streaked horny face. The thing raised its head in surprise as usual, and the arrows flew. Saran's hit it just above the chest; about five feet low; but the other two crossbow bolts hit it in the throat perfectly.

The sivilin shrieked and clawed at its neck before giving chase but it was too late. The three klutes were already falling safely toward the forest a couple thousand feet below. They adjusted their fall so they were angled toward a mile long set of thick timber that lay over a steep hill about four miles north of the colony.

The sivilin was giving chase, but was safely behind when they flared for an entrance beneath the canopy of branches. There was a foot trail here that was familiar to all of them and they jogged up the path using their wings at times to propel them forward at a quicker pace when the undergrowth permitted. They were a few miles south of the treehouses but they'd gathered wood and foodstuffs in the forest here many times.

Arak realized that they probably resembled a bunch of birds emulating broken wings to lead a predator away from their nest and he began laughing out loud.

"What's so funny?" Shandra was running in front of him with partially folded wings and she glanced back.

"Oh nothing." He answered. "I bet we look like a bunch of sadagaudies hopping along pretending we have broken wings trying lead a taral, or moolara away from a ground nest."

Shandra and Saran both burst with laughter then. They realized they were safe now and they slowed the pace to a walk when they came to a small trickling spring.

Arak glanced back at Saran and complimented her. "That was an amazing shot for your first time."

Shandra spoke from behind as they strolled up a faint game trail. "I completely missed my first shot at one of them, and you fell with us perfectly in the intersect dive."

It was a nice place for them to fly up through the canopy along the small stream if the giant flying lizard followed them up the trail so they were in no hurry. The branches would be way too close together for the wings of a sivilin to break through and they would be able to escape just as they'd done the previous week.

They waited about an hour before they decided to take a look, and Arak was the first to go up through the canopy. He landed on a big branch about three quarters of the way up a two a hundred foot pine that stuck up above the nearby forest. He scanned the countryside carefully but there was no sign of any sivilin. He whistled loudly and the two females flew up out of the narrow break in the trees gaining altitude with a slight degree of difficulty. He joined them and they headed back toward the Thunder cliffs where they found a rising column of warmer air. It didn't take them long to reach three quarters timberline and they decided to go back to the lookout post for awhile.

Saran was so excited she couldn't stop talking about the incident. She was amazed and dumbfounded by the dauntless act of crossbow marksmanship that she'd just witnessed. Students weren't even supposed to take sivilin hunting lessons until they'd been out of the academy for at least two years and then they would just accompany hunting parties and observe while practicing unarmed terminal dives for at least several encounters.

Question followed question, and she paced from one side of the rock shelter to the other side while glancing up at the sky. Within half an hour she knew all about Arak and Shandra's adventures from the past couple of weeks. The only thing she didn't know was how devastating the big quad bladed arrows were.

Miz was able to eat some solid food now, but she was covered with blisters and pimples like most of the ill in the main cavern. Her fever was gone now, and she was able to move around in the three room dwelling with no problem. She stayed busy making candles. She was an expert and knew just how long to melt the chura tallow and exactly how much beeswax to add. The beekeepers were all incapacitated, but she had a supply of wax from the summer before. She was still too weak to attempt flying and she still had a nagging cough.

Shandra's parents were unable to exert themselves at all, but their cliff dwelling was next to Miz's in the cliff just across Froze to Death creek from the main cavern. Duroon, or other friends looked in on them at least three or four times a day.

The students that didn't get the virus just kept bringing firewood and fresh water for anyone that needed it. Arak and Shandra shrugged the sickness off with no secondary symptoms or blisters for some reason, but anyone else that had come down with the pneumonia seemed to have serious near death relapses whenever they exerted themselves. All of the elders and colony leaders excluding Duroon were still incapacitated with the disease so Arak and Shandra just ignored Nooney's or Magahila's warnings about flying out of the canyon in any direction due to the danger of sivilin.

Of Arak and Shandra's immediate class Rhee, Dulles, and Enneka had contracted the disease and were bed-ridden. Saran and Tillery had shrugged off the illness but the other half of the graduating class was down with the high fever and suffocating mucus.

A sivilin flew up through the pass about mid-morning and the three sixteen year old students quickly loaded their modified crossbows with their newly crafted quad bladed arrows. They left the lookout post and were out over the canyon in just a few minutes. Arak could see the creature a couple of miles from them. It was already about six thousand vertical feet below the lookout shelter, and it looked like it was heading for the colony. Arak was worried that it might spot the small chalow herd. They pulled with all their strength to overtake the sivilin and when it began circling they folded their wings most of the way and dropped rapidly toward an intercept.

They fell silently in front of the creature and as always it raised its head in surprise and gave a quick backward sweep with its wings. The arrows all hit it in the neck, but only Shandra's appeared to hit it in the throat. Arak's arrow was slightly higher and went in under the jaw and Saran's was a few feet below Shandra's.

The beast was enraged and dove after the three klutes, but it was a half mile behind when they leveled off over the thick forest north of Sagitar. It gave up pursuit almost as soon as it lost sight of the klutes.

They stood in the thick timbered valley and relaxed for a few minutes while walking around and peering up expectantly through the foliage. Birds and insects were chirping in their undisturbed manner, busy in their own small worlds; completely unaware of dramas that were unfolding on a higher level of intelligence or plane of existence.

Arak looked at Shandra. "I hope we don't ever have to escape from one where there's no ground cover."

"Yes. Me too." She answered. "They have designated areas in the Desowan, huge khiska thickets; some nice forested canyons out there, but not like this one."

"No one except for the chalow herder has ever been killed on the ground that I know of." Said Saran. "But we aren't allowed to witness hunting images yet. There might be some attacks that the sivilin hunters don't ever share."

Arak sat down and leaned back against a tree. "My father said one of his friends was killed on the ground. There was no cover and four of them had to split up when a sivilin dove down at them from above a broken cloud ceiling. It followed one of them around a mesa and caught him before he could find a place to hide. I was only four years old. I've never actually seen the images. I just overheard my father talking about the incident a couple of times over the years. It was very graphic and there wasn't a body to bring back."

"I can't wait until we can explore out there." Said Shandra.

"I'm still trying to imprint the images that I just witnessed. I don't want to leave anything out when we get to share in the gathering cathedral." She laughed. "We will surely be in big trouble; probably punished indefinitely."

"We are going to need more obsidian." Said Shandra. "I'm about out of it at home."

"My father has a whole storage bin full of blanks and glass cores that we brought from The Glass Canyon." Arak stood up and stretched his arms above his head. "I'll bring some up to the shelter tomorrow."

"We probably wasted a few more arrows today." Shandra opened her quiver and began counting her quad bladed shafts.

"It's never a waste." Arak replied. "If nothing else that particular sivilin might not come over the mountains again, and we probably kept if from getting a chalow." He laughed. "But I know you are getting tired of making them."

The three of them returned to the top of Mount Sagitar and spent the rest of the day working on their weapons.

A weak cold front brewed up a huge lightning storm that blew in off of the Desowan that evening.

They were safely in the canyon before it rolled over the mountain and unleashed its fury dumping heavy rain and even some small hail. Arak and Shandra made their rounds checking in on everybody and ate fresh mikta steak that had been killed by some of the students that had been gathering wood that day.

They spent an hour with Shandra's parents after dinner. They were inquisitive when Shandra mentioned something about the lookout post on top of Sagitar, but they didn't try to pry into private memories and remained ignorant of any sivilin hunting. They were both feeling much better but still very weak and covered with suppurating blisters from head to foot.

Enneka was still down with a high fever and Miz was about the same as Shandra's parents. They spent the night in Arak's room on the wide webbing of his stretched cot. The dreams came again and a very strange phenomenon occurred. Neither Arak or Shandra believed in the occult or any kind of supernatural contingency, but when they were both awakened by nightmares at about midnight they realized that there might be some kind of sanctity or higher power that they just didn't comprehend. Although they were unable to share rem sleep dream images they were still able to compare nightmares verbally while they were fresh in their mindset, and it was obvious that the two of them had been having exactly the same dream.

Arak had experienced the nightmare several times. It was the same one he'd had the last time he'd handled the ancient ceremonial arrows. Shandra turned on her side and looked at him. They were laying on soft Zinda fur and were warm beneath a spotted light weight taral comforter.

"I Just had the strangest dream." She said softly.

"I was dreaming about sivilin hunting again." He answered. "The same dream I told you about the other day. I have it over and over."

"I know." She pulled back the taral covering and poured water from a small vase on the table next to the bed. "I just shot the sivilin in the back of the head too."

The dreams came and went all night but they both slept well after the initial shared nightmare. Most of Arak's dreams were about sivilin hunting, but Shandra said she even had one where she was visiting the Mocktaw islands or some other place south of the Taro colony. Someplace where there was a nice sandy beach with fish frying over a fire.

They dropped down to the main cavern and found Duroon and Saran about daylight. Saran's parents were both in a high adobe brick walled cliff dwelling east of the main cavern, and they were mending slightly, but they needed help cooking and making medicated broths. They both had blisters in their throats, and were having trouble eating. Saran said she was going to make them an anti inflammatory herbal broth, then she would visit Shandra and Arak on the mountain later.

The first sivilin came over the mountain about midmorning. They did their usual stalk on the creature but it heard them or sensed them for some reason. The two klutes were about a hundred yards above it when it suddenly looked back at them. Luckily it just stared at them for a moment instead of changing direction. They both rolled over and quickly aborted the attack. The dive for the forest was successful but this particular sivilin was close behind, and it followed them up the trail crashing through the brush and saplings for a few hundred yards. The klutes took flight then and left it stuck beneath the upper canopy of branches.

Arak and Shandra circled a weak thermal back up along the Thunder cliffs before the thing figured out they were gone. Another of the creatures was visible over the colony now, and they were in a quandary as it dipped a wing and side slipped toward the steppes below the Moon Creek divide and of course the chalow herd.

"Let's try to put some arrows into it." Said Arak. They were circling upward on in a small column of rising warm air. Arak was almost straight across from Shandra making verbal communication easy in a loud tone of voice.

"Let's cross the valley and try to get above the chalow steppes then." She answered as she glanced down and back. The sivilin that had followed them into the forest was about a mile below them and safely out of reach for the time being. Arak could see where it had trampled half of a small sapling grove before taking flight. When they reached timberline he left the thermal and headed for the Moon creek divide and hopefully an intercept. Shandra flew up next to him and reloaded her crossbow.

"We can fire our arrows and drop into the trees between Tempest and Froze to Death." Said Arak.

Shandra pointed. "Look! It has killed a chalow, and it's just taking off. We have plenty of time."

They crossed the canyon quickly and put themselves over a place that would intersect their flight path with that of the sivilin, then they began their dive. The creature didn't hear them and they dropped in front of it about three miles up the canyon from the colony. They were near Tempest mountain when arrows flew and another sivilin had two more knife bladed missiles lodged deep in its esophagus.

The second sivilin was coming across the canyon now and it seemed disoriented or confused with all of the commotion and shrieking. The dead chalow fell to earth on the sandy shoreline of a deep mountain lake about a mile from where the klutes entered the thickest forest between Tempest and Froze to Death peaks. It was actually called Froze to Death lake. Gigantic blackened petrified sivilin bones had been discovered just above the lake when the main glacier in the canyon had receded one summer and revealed them. It was only about four miles up the canyon from the main cave.

Both of the sivilin broke off the attack, and after hiding in the pine canyon for about an hour the two klutes flew back down to Sagitar and found Saran. She said someone had heard the wounded sivilin fly over the canyon raising a din, but they didn't know what had caused it. By the time they had walked outside for a look the flying beast was out of sight up the canyon somewhere beyond the edge of Froze to Death mountain.

The chalow herds were running wild now with no supervision whatsoever. No one had seen Arak, Shandra, or Saran dive on any of the creatures even though they had been in plain sight of the colony at times.

No more sivilin were sighted from the lookout post that day, and the three klutes stayed busy making weapons until late in the afternoon.

Two young visitors from the Taro colony arrived that evening and brought news of the epidemic, A few of the older generation were getting over the virus, but they were still too weak to fly. Mik and Jarek had been lucky and hadn't contracted the disease in Taro. They were glad to see that almost everyone in Sagitar was still alive and recovering. They were worried about the sivilin coming over the mountains even though they hadn't seen any near Taro. They said some sivilin hunters from the southern colony should be able to move to Sagitar to help repel the creatures in a couple of weeks; maybe even sooner.

The next morning another sivilin flew up over the pass between Thunder and Sagitar. It was only about fifty feet above the scree sloped plateau when it came up out of the Desowan and banked to the north fighting a rotary flow from a strong breeze. The wind was causing an immediate downdraft on the west slope. The creature whipped its tail and tilted sideways one way, then the other before it stabilized its glide. It was about a quarter mile from the pass when it began a slow descent.

The sivilin was completely unaware of Arak, Shandra, and Saran until it had three crossbow bolts imbedded in its neck. The huge winged creature put up a noisy halfhearted chase, but it was two miles behind when the klutes entered the forest in their favorite place south of the treehouses.

The sivilin flew right over the treehouses, but it stayed about a thousand feet above the ground. It let out a couple of ear shattering screeching sounds as it flew over, then it disappeared up the canyon somewhere north of the Thunder cliffs.

Arak Shandra and Saran compared images and were happy with their marksmanship. All three of their arrows had hit within a foot of each other. The final image that Arak shared showed the black feathered fletchings in small a upside down triangle just below the creature's jaw. Arak and Shandra both complimented Saran on her improved marksmanship.

Some of the younger students happened to be coming down the canyon loaded with firewood, and they saw the wounded sivilin circling down toward the canyon floor. Arak, Shandra, and Saran were already out of sight.

They met up with the younger class awhile later when everyone came out of hiding. The juvenile group of students were aged from eleven to not quite fifteen years, and they were very excited to actually see a sivilin up so close. They were a motley group. Arak could tell their mothers and fathers were ill. Some of them were definitely in need of a trip to the hot springs and a set of clean clothes.

They'd all touched down together in a grassy clearing, and as always they were glad for any excuse to take a break from their chores. The group enjoyed the warm sunlight of the clear day while sharing a few snacks. The leader was a young male named Jayko, and he looked at Arak, Shandra, and

Saran inquisitively. He could see by their heavily loaded quivers that they were hunting and not ferrying firewood.

"We haven't seen any mikta or chura today." He said. "But there were a couple of mikta bucks up the canyon about half an hour north of here a few days ago. None of us had a weapon. Nooney and Tillary said we should just carry wood and not waste any time hunting from now on."

Shandra laughed and addressed the younger student. "Nooney is kind of stressed out these days. I don't see why some of you can't carry weapons. The ice caves still have some frozen meat, but we will need to stock up a little bit for next winter."

Saran spoke up. "The sivilin are killing everything. There used to be a few big herds of chura north of here. Even some prairie chura. Now there is nothing but moolara and sprites. Orem said the zinda that used to prowl the canyon from time to time have even disappeared."

One of the younger students pointed toward the north face of Froze to Death mountain. The rugged granite sluiced peak rose ominously almost godlike in shadow, its four apex towers angled outward toward the canyon in a sinister manner.

"Someone said they thought they saw another dead sivilin over by Froze to Death last night." He said. "They said there's more than one carcass over in the trees now. We flew up along the timberline this morning and looked around but couldn't find it. We didn't look very hard." He laughed. "Phew. They sure stink. Nobody would go near the last one we found."

No one spoke for a moment then Jayko began shrugging into his wood laden pack. We better get this load to Duroon." He looked around at his small group. "I wonder what is killing the sivilin."

"Who cares. Maybe that one caught something from Sory when it killed her." Su-Lin was usually kind of shy, and she spoke up for the first time since Arak had touched down in the meadow. She was only twelve years old and her pack looked a little bit too heavy for her slim wings for some reason. She let one of the other students adjust the straps above them. "One of them killed my father last year. I hope they all die slow suffering deaths."

That afternoon Arak was looking through the small window in the lookout shelter. The wind was coming in from the east about twenty miles an hour. A weak breeze for the top of Sagitar. There were puffy broken clouds over the Desowan at about ten thousand feet. He thought it might be fun to soar amongst them while playing hide and seek or tag with a group of students. It was a fun game they'd played since their first flying days. They had different rules and games. Sometimes they would have teams and use telepathy to send images to their teammates. There were even games that required boundaries made by landmarks below.

A sivilin came in over the pass south of Sagitar that afternoon. It was coming from the west this time and it caught the three klutes completely off guard. By the time anyone saw it the thing had flown two miles out over the Desowan foothills. They left it alone for several reasons. It was flying into the wind and Arak doubted if they could catch up with it soon enough to find a safe haven. They'd only been over the Desowan a few times and didn't know the area that well. They weren't sure of safe landing zones or hiding places more than a couple of miles from the mountains. Arak's father had told him there were a lot of small caves and crevasses to hide in that were safe, but Arak had no idea where any of them were.

They sat and watched it fly effortlessly out over the Desowan. A magnificent creature probably capable of wiping out all intelligent life on the planet.

Shandra was sitting next to Arak peering out of the small port in the east wall. "We need to go exploring out there more so we can find some places to hide." She said absent mindedly. She still had the arrow she'd been working on in her hand and she pointed it out the window as if aiming for a shot.

"We will have plenty of years for that." Arak laughed. "We better stick to harassing the ones coming from out there until someone takes us hunting in the Desowan and gives us some landmarks."

"I know where there is one place." Said Saran. "But my father said its two hours glide from the pass. There's a huge mesa on the other side of the closest deep canyon that runs to the sea. There's even a pond or lake near the top. It's very rugged along the base where fallen rock has created underground passages and natural bridges."

She closed her eyes and Arak and Shandra both followed suit to receive the second hand images they knew she would send. Imaging skills were returning slowly after their slight fevers had subsided, and they could send and receive easily as long as they were in each other's presence.

The telepathic signals were fuzzy as were most relayed images but Arak could see the mesa and the canyon. The rocky slope with dozens of huge jumbled leaning slabs was on the east side. They centered on the stream of images from Saran until her father had dropped to the ground and walked into a long passageway with a narrow entrance.

"My father said there's lots of places like this in the Desowan and hiding after an attack is usually not a problem."

She opened her eyes and Arak looked at her and nodded. "I've seen images of some of my parent's favorite places too."

They were getting ready to head for the main cavern when Saran spotted another sivilin coming in from the northeast. It flew up beside Thunder and soared the ridge lift along the pass straight toward them. The thing turned its head down and back to the right several times as if looking for something and passed within a hundred yards of the lookout shelter. The three klutes waited a few minutes until it was farther south along the mountain range and they struck out after it. They gained altitude rapidly with strong ridge lift and were soon a couple thousand feet above the narrow rugged granite ridge that jutted up and ran south from Sagitar for about five miles. Smaller peaks loomed ahead and some of them were named.

There was Pyramid mountain on the other side of the river just south of the grass and brushy chalow steppes. There was Scree mountain about five miles straight south of mount Sagitar, and two twin conjoined peaks just south of Pyramid were called Mawl mountain.

The sivilin continued to soar southwest toward Pyramid mountain using the east wind to provide easy gliding. Soon the three klutes were well above it in a good position for an attack. Arak hesitated and motioned to Saran and Shandra to wait. He was afraid to attack so close to the near vertical slopes along Pyramid mountain for fear of escaping safely.

Suddenly the thing banked to the left and began flying back across the canyon toward Skree mountain. When Arak was sure he could reach terminal velocity safely he made a motion with his hand and they began their assault. The sivilin was completely unaware of the klutes, and the attack was a complete success.

The three of them dropped into thick deep forest downriver from the steppes and Pyramid mountain. They were unscathed as usual, and the enraged sivilin gave up chase about two thousand feet above the canyon floor while clawing at its neck. The teenagers were becoming very prolific in their silent attacks. None of them had missed a shot for over a week now and they were making razor sharp obsidian serrated arrow points with an expertise achieved by only a few individuals in the klute city. The small saw bladed knives were hard to make.

The weather remained nice for a few days so the three youngsters just kept making arrows and harassing the sivilin.

As the days slowly passed students gathering firewood, plants, fruits, and herbs had come across a few gigantic sivilin carcasses laying in strange places throughout the Sagitarian canyon and its side branches. No one was sure what they were dying from, and only a few instances had ever been witnessed where the giant flying lizards were fighting each other.

Mawls were the giveaway in open country. Whenever something was laying dead for a few days the large feathered scavengers would home in along with smaller competition; some feathered and some furred

The drier weeks of summer weren't usually a dangerous time for lightning storms, but whenever it got very hot over the Desowan the storms would build up. One day Arak, Shandra, and Saran were driven off of the mountain by another dangerous storm. The cumulonimbus clouds rose to heights unobtainable by sivilin or klutes. The top of this particular storm had boiled upwards for nine or ten miles, and it came over the mountains as usual. They spent the day visiting friends and relatives.

Some of the ill were starting to walk around each day. As long as they didn't over exert themselves they continued healing. The few that tried to fly or do chores that required strenuous physical activity always relapsed back into the fever or mucus stages of the disease.

The day after the severe storm the air was fresh and crisp. The gigantic supercell had long since passed over. The sun was up and not hardly a cloud could be seen from horizon to horizon in any direction.

Arak saw the sivilin almost as soon as he removed his pack and put it beside the lookout post. He left it where it was and pointed to the northeast. Shandra and Saran could see the flying beast as it slowly climbed up and over the pass; huge wings beating rhythmically in the calm morning air. The three of them waited for it to fly over the divide, and when it banked unexpectedly to the south they hid behind the wall of the small shelter. It was about half a mile from them when it flew past and started out across the canyon toward Pyramid mountain.

The three of them waited another minute or so and then they began their chase. They dropped on the sivilin after they were across the river and were successful. All three of their arrows hit the thing in the upper throat and it immediately began shrieking. It dove after them in a frenzy while clawing at its neck and throat.

After Arak pulled the trigger he began his inverted dive. He looked back up between his feet at the wounded sivilin. They were safely out of reach now; Shandra on his left and Saran on his right. He noticed something out of the corner of his eye that disturbed him. There was another of the creatures dropping from the other side of the canyon, and it was coming toward them at an incredible speed. He pointed and the other two soon saw the second sivilin.

They dropped into the thickest part of mixed forest between Pyramid mountain and the Sagitarian river then made their way toward the northwest for a few minutes mostly on foot. There was a small clearing nearby and the sivilin landed. They heard the wounded creature crashing through branches behind them. It was furious and shrieking like some of the others that had been wounded similarly. The three klutes continued on through the shadows cast by the thick canopy of upper branches trying to gain distance.

A small herd of miktas spooked and disappeared into the undergrowth ahead of them just before they came to another tiny clearing where they could take flight easily without striking limbs. Arak led the way and rose about a hundred and fifty feet up out of the gloom into the upper canopy.

He was leery and grabbed a high branch. He found another for his foot before leaving the trees completely and it was a good thing he did. The second sivilin was only about a quarter mile from them and was skimming the treetops toward the river. Shandra and Saran had followed his lead and they both stood on branches just below him. It was so close that Arak could see where it was missing part of its right wing. A big triangular slice was missing about a third of the way from its wing tip.

"The other one is right over there skimming the trees." Said Arak just loud enough for them to hear. "It's off to the south about a quarter mile."

The three of them stood motionlessly for about five minutes watching and waiting. The wounded sivilin had finally stopped thrashing around but the other one was still flying nearby in wide spiraling circles about a hundred feet above the trees.

Arak's legs were starting to get a pins and needles sensation from standing as motionless as possible when the monster finally left the chase and started upriver. It was still early morning but the warm sunlight was already causing thermals to rise from the rocky canyon floor below mount Sagitar. The sivilin caught an updraft and was five thousand feet above the river ten minutes later.

"It's finally gone." Arak glanced down at the other two. "I guess we're safe for the time being. Phew; I can smell the other one in the forest."

Shandra climbed the branch next to him pushing leaves out of the way and peered up at the vanishing sivilin. She grimaced.

"It smells like dead fish that have been laying on a river bank for a week." She said. "They've never chased us like that. When did it come over the pass?"

"It must have come up out of the Desowan while we were getting ready to drop on the first one." Replied Arak quietly. "I thought we scanned the sky before we started the chase. We'd better be more careful."

"It's going past the colony toward Thunder but it's high." She spoke quietly. "I hope it goes up the canyon."

Arak shifted his weight and stretched his wings outward. "Let's go back up to the shelter. We can fly downriver and catch an updraft before we get in the shadow of Pyramid."

Arak flew upriver and checked behind them for the wounded sivilin but there was no sign of the creature. They all circled upward on a weak thermal over the rocky foothills and granite sluiced terrain along the west face of mount Sagitar. The thermal played out about half way up the side of the mountain so they used an incoming eastward breeze to give them ridge lift up to the pass between Sagitar and Thunder mountain.

Shandra saw the monster first, and yelled a warning. It was coming around the north side of Thunder and it had already spotted them. The sivilin looked gigantic and it appeared to be missing part of its wing just like the one that had been circling over the forest.

No one said anything; they just plummeted for the forest south of the treehouses. The sivilin was close behind, and chased them all the way to the ground this time, but the three klutes were about a half mile ahead when they started up the trail through the trees. The huge flying lizard came down and followed them up the trail, and it was amazingly quick for such a large beast. It followed them clear up the trail to the treehouse.

The thing looked up at them with big golden eyes and switched its tail like a gigantic zinda. It hissed loudly, and cut loose with a long deafening shriek that echoed throughout the nearby forest. It was less than fifty yards from the three young hunters, and its stench permeated the area. They all fired their bows at the same time. Quad bladed arrows flew, and all of the missiles struck the enraged sivilin either in the mouth or upper neck.

They abandoned the tree house as soon as they shot their arrows and flew up through a small opening in the upper canopy of mixed deciduous and pines. The enraged sivilin began lurching up the big pine tree behind them, but was unable to get its wings spread due to thick branches that almost spanned the upper canopy of forest.

They heard it demolishing the tree house as they began flying north skimming the treetops. Arak kept glancing backward, but there was no sign of the monster. They were soon safely up the canyon between Thunder and Froze to Death. They decided to leave this particular sivilin alone, and when they were about half an hour's glide up the canyon they hid in the pines. The canyon was deep and narrow with near vertical terrain on both sides. A two mile long lake lay in the center. It was called Rainbow lake and the fishing was good for the remainder of the day.

CHAPTER TEN

The river was wide and slow moving; dark with sediment. Cin flew slowly over the stream and checked the ground cover beyond. There were at least two species of miktas here. He'd been seeing small herds of the deer for three days now. He'd gradually left behind the deciduous swampland and its myriad of waterways and tangled jungles. He was sure this was the Desowan river; it was almost half a mile across.

He'd been searching for a neural signal, but the wave rifts were completely silent. If this was the Desowan river he should be able to follow it north for a few days and come to a landmark known to the klutes as the Desowan Gates. The granite out-cropping rose a couple thousand feet from the valley floor and jutted outward toward the west from a low lying flat topped forested mountain range. A huge three hundred mile long lake called Sivilin lake should be north of there and he would be able to follow it west for at least a hundred miles. Somehow over the eons as the planet's crust had twisted and succumbed to upheaval the river had sustained and eroded a channel through the granite wall.

Cin had only seen three sivilin in the past week, but lightning storms were relentless in their after-noon and evening occurrences. Some of them were so severe he had to fly many miles out of his way to stay safe. He saw his first tornado one afternoon and had to wait out a huge wall cloud that had mush-roomed upward above his flight path. He examined the devastating effects of the funnel cloud and could barely believe his eyes. The forest looked like kin-dling with nothing but a wide swath ten of foot snags sticking upward where there had been hundred and fifty foot trees. He was hard pressed making it a hundred miles in a day sometimes, but living off the land was easy here and provided a diet of variety. The forests were teeming with small game, wildfowl, and fruit trees so he didn't kill a mikta.

He realized that this would be a safe place to relocate for awhile if they couldn't deter the sivilin over the Desowan or the delta. The elders had even suggested it at one time, but the majority of the klute population had wanted to stay near the mountains.

He flew almost effortlessly upriver all morning staying low; enjoying the thick humid air on the warm summer day. He was relieved to finally be in a familiar place even though he was still many hundreds of miles from Sagitar. A couple days later he flew over the Desowan Gates and watched the water pour over the giant sluice like falls.

The lake lay beyond and he felt a sudden overpowering feeling of relief. He'd been flying for weeks in strange unmapped territories not ever quite sure where he was. Cin was home. He'd been to the other side of the lake before, and he'd seen images of the falls. It was only about two hundred miles to the Desowan wasteland from here and he pushed to the west along the lakefront.

Thunderstorms were still frequent, especially around the lake and he had to seek refuge from the lightning that afternoon, but he made good progress. He caught fish from a stream that drained into the lake and was able to use his firestarting materials to cook them that evening.

Cin continued westward the next morning. He cooked fish and a moolara and smoked them for two days. He wanted jerky in his pack before crossing the Desowan. He knew he would come across more sivilin in the wasteland so he would fly at night most of the time if he could avoid lightning. He flew along the southern lakeshore and watched for chura but failed to sight any of the larger antlered species that preferred the muskeg areas and damp forests around water. Two days later he soared above broken clouds and left the friendly lake and its bounty of nourishment behind. The country west was becoming more and more sparsely timbered or forested with long open clearings. It was noticeably drier here and grass was already brown and headed out preparing to seed.

A sivilin made an appearance the second day after he left the lake. Cin was just below a broken cloud ceiling hopping thermals or cloud surfing the westward air flow with little physical effort. He was at about timberline and the huge flying lizard passed below him a few thousand feet above the ground. It never saw him but it was a definite awakening and he sharpened his senses.

Lightning storms were still frequent even in the drier climate and he usually had to give wide berth to at least one storm every day. It was hot, and frontal systems were always moving up from the south with very high humidity. Sometimes thunderstorm outflow or inflow caused by downdrafts or updrafts would blow him far to the north or south at fifty or sixty miles an hour but he stayed his course toward the west.

A few days later Cin crossed over a fairly large grass fire that had been started by lightning. He guessed he was making way more than a hundred miles a day, but zig zagging around storms was hindering his progress. He recognized a landmark when he neared one particular rock formation. The huge pointed rocky projection rose three or four thousand feet from the surrounding arid countryside and it even had a name. The sivilin hunters had simply christened it Cloud point. He'd been there half a dozen times.

It was good to be back in the Desowan even though he was seeing at least one sivilin a day. Cin might be in Sagitar in three days if the weather permitted, and the important memories of his journey would be shared and even written down in the archive scrolls for future generations.

CHAPTER ELEVEN

Enneka was still ill, but he was able to walk around. He was afraid to glide down to the main cavern for fear of exerting himself on the way back up to his family's dwelling. He looked funny with pimples all over his face and was even the subject for some teasing. They missed him on the sivilin hunts, but Shandra and Saran were both expert shots now. They were dropping on at least one sivilin almost every day, sometimes two, and one rare day they put arrows into three of the flying monsters and escaped all of them unscathed. One of the three had been near mount Sagitar but out over the Desowan.

More students had flown in from the south and they were bringing good news. Many of the adults that had acquired the disease in Taro were flying now, but the virus had attacked the southern cities two or three weeks before it had made it to Sagitar. Not any of the adults in the Sagitarian colony were able to fly yet. Only a very few that hadn't been ill to start with.

Students gathering wood and foodstuffs said there were at least nine dead sivilin laying around in the canyon within five or six miles of Sagitar. No one knew what was killing them and a rumor had started that the sivilin were getting the sickness like the klutes.

Arak, Shandra, and Saran kept attacking them from their lookout station. They didn't say anything about hunting sivilin to anyone. They wondered how many were dying from their arrows but they didn't examine any carcasses; they just didn't have time. They actually wondered if the rumors of the sickness were true. If so then there would be dead sivilin everywhere, and no one had even checked the canyon south of the city.

Some of the wood gathering students had found a new carcass below the east side of Froze to Death mountain the day before the Taro visitors had arrived. They'd noticed a place near the sluiced granite face where the tops of a bunch of pine trees were all knocked off. They'd gone for a look and had found another dead sivilin.

Shandra had noticed an ominous circling of mawls off the eastern foothills below Pyramid mountain one day when she'd left the lookout post by herself, and they'd seen another gathering of the scavenging birds in the trees between the river and Scree mountain one morning before they had launched another attack. It was possible that there were dead sivilin in this area also.

About four weeks after the viral pandemic had plunged the colony into a helpless state it began to subside. Adults were starting to walk around in the main cavern now and even some of the elders were beginning to tell jokes and sit around the cooking fires pitching in when needed.

It was past midsummer now and most of the snow was gone from the nearby peaks. Another week slowly passed, and Arak, Shandra and Saran continued diving on sivilin in the canyon whenever weather permitted, and whenever the flying nemesis came over the divide.

Students ferrying wood now confirmed at least a dozen sivilin corpses scattered throughout the north end of the canyon between Thunder and Froze to Death mountain.

The three youngsters were sitting outside of the stone shelter on top of Mount Sagitar one evening discussing Nooney's problems when a lone sivilin came in from the south. It flew by the shelter about a half mile west of them and just kept going north. For some reason it didn't even look down and they were relieved.

"I'm getting so I don't like diving on them." Said Arak as he put his crossbow and quiver back down. "Someday one of them is going to do something unpredictable and somebody is going to get hurt; I have a bad feeling."

Shandra reassured him. "We should have help soon. Maybe even tomorrow or the next day. Mik said there are sivilin hunters coming. The best from Taro are able to fly again according to him, and it's only a three day hop from there to Sagitar. One and a half from the Baden River colony, but he said they are still in the recovery process there."

"I hope you're right." Answered Arak. "It seems like we are getting awfully lucky. Not one of us has had a scratch yet except for tree branches. That one that followed us to the tree house gave me the creeps though."

Saran laughed. "Yeah, me too. And that's not entirely true. I have a pretty bad cut on my arm from that one we shot over on the north side of Thunder a couple days ago. I guess you're still right though; it's from a tree branch."

"You're dreams scare me." Said Shandra. "Especially that one we shared. I try not to think about them, but if you think you're having a premonition we'd better be extra careful until help gets here from down south."

Saran stood and looked at her and Arak. Her dark hair blew to the side in the breeze. "That was kind of weird when you said you had the same dream that night. When the sivilin hunters get here let's go check some of the dead carcasses that are scattered around. Let's see if any of them have arrows in their necks."

"That's a good idea." Arak smiled at her. "Duroon will probably just make us carry firewood anyway."

"Orem is a lot better now." Shandra stood up and stretched her legs. "He asked me if we'd been hunting. I just said yes. He'll be surprised to see all of our attacks at an image sharing someday. I just hope everyone gets their memory recall back. I miss going to the image sharings, and you're mother always lets us sneak a little of her wine."

Arak stood up and put the arrowpoint he'd been working on down on the wicker table that they'd moved outside on the calm day. "We must have dropped on over twenty sivilin in the last few weeks."

"More like two dozen." Said Shandra. "I've sort of been keeping track."

"And all of them have arrows in them too." Said Saran. "The only one I missed was that time when my crossbow bolt wasn't notched properly."

"I think we all had a miss or two." Said Shandra. "And that one over by Skree mountain didn't raise its head very far when we dropped past. But you're right. All of the sivilin were hit with at least two arrows; usually three."

"The one that followed us up the trail to the treehouse scared me too." Shandra went on. "We never found that one. I think two arrows went into its mouth."

"Yeah." Answered Arak. "And it was able to climb the tree after it wrecked the shelter and fly up out of the forest. Luckily we were long gone."

They put away their tools and obsidian, then hoisted their small packs. Arak launched himself into the slight breeze coming from the Desowan. The other two were right behind and they banked over the divide and took the light evening katabatic flow down off of the mountains.

It was dinner time in the main cavern when they arrived, and they were very relieved; almost ecstatic to see a few middle aged newcomers from Taro. They were even more relieved to hear that there were more on the way. They were all sivilin hunters and had been out over the Desowan dozens of times.

Orem and Duroon were busy talking to them so Arak, Shandra and Saran just waved to assure them that they were done for the day with whatever duties they'd been performing. They ate with Nooney at the schooling cavern and went to their separate dwellings. Arak was glad that his mother had finally stopped coughing. She had prepared a meal for herself out of mikta steak and wild summer fruits and vegetables that had been brought by students.

The next morning there was a big group of people sitting around in the main cavern listening to Duroon and Orem talking to the sivilin hunters from Taro. Arak, Shandra, and Saran all took seats and listened to them discuss strategies and plans for the day. Of the graduating class Yas and Tillary were the only two that could fly, and they were still looking after parents and close relatives when they weren't busy helping Nooney. Rhee and Dulles were getting over their virus and they were present, but still not able to fly long distances. Kneviel, and Swope were in the back watching but they were unable to do tasks that required any physical strength at all, and Enneka was still up with his parents.

Savant made an appearance and joined the discussion for awhile but he was still having trouble doing any kind of activities that required strength or stamina. The sivilin hunters from Taro were led by a very experienced individual. His name was Mace and he was almost a legend in the profession. He'd been in on at least nine or ten confirmed kills over the past couple of years. There were six sivilin hunters in all, and they decided to ridge soar the pass along Thunder mountain until reinforcements arrived. That was the easiest and most frequent place for sivilin to come over the mountains.

When they were done visiting and exchanging images from Taro the group of sivilin hunters strolled formidably to the mouth of the cave with their weapons. They wore carefully tailored leather clothing that wouldn't flap or rustle so they could freefall silently in strong winds. Some of them had belts adorned with zinda or bront claws.

Mace suddenly noticed Arak, Shandra, and Saran standing beside a nearby fire. The three students looked strange to him for some reason. They had worn crossbows that appeared to need new strings, and quivers that showed much use. Their bare arms and faces were scratched from tree branches and their clothing was also ragged and tattered almost to a shambles.

Mace walked past the trio and was almost to the launching ramp next to the stairway of the cave entrance when he suddenly stopped and turned back toward Arak as if scrutinizing him. "And just what is it that you youngsters do for the colony?"

Arak looked at him and then glanced at Saran and Shandra for a moment before answering. "We hunt mostly."

Shandra smiled at Arak, then addressed Mace. "Yes we have been doing a lot of hunting lately."

"Well it looks like you could use some new bow strings." He said. "How has the chura hunting been around here? The sivilin have killed most of them down south over the past year or so but there's still a lot of miktas."

"We haven't killed any miktas or chura for quite awhile." Arak answered. "But there have been a lot of sivilin coming over the mountains. We've been watching for them from a lookout shelter on top of Mount Sagitar."

"Hahahahah!" Mace laughed loudly and the rest of his companions joined in. "What was the purpose? You students don't actually think you could hunt sivilin do you? That bow doesn't even look like it has a fifty pound pull."

Arak didn't really know what to say. "One of the chalow herders was killed here in Sagitar while on the ground, so we decided to watch for them and warn the city."

Shandra spoke up again. "Yes, we did see a lot come over the mountains, but they only got two or three chalows on the ridge up behind here. No one else was killed."

"We fixed up an old ancient stone shelter." Said Saran. "It's on top of Mount Sagitar. You can't miss it. It's a good spot to sit and watch if you don't want to fly out over the Desowan."

Mace didn't answer. He just looked up toward the summit of the snow streaked mountain.

"You youngsters be careful now." One of Mace's friends addressed them as he followed the rest of the group to the stairway and launch ramp. "If you see any sivilin get out of the sky."

The hunters from Taro lifted off and flew slowly down the valley toward the river. The sun was shining on the upper half of Thunder and Sagitar with a faint rose colored tint and it was already warming the early morning air in the lower canyon.

"We should have given them some arrows." Said Sandra.

"It wouldn't do any good." Arak glanced at her. "The grooves in their bows are too narrow. Let's go look at the dead sivilin down by Pyramid mountain and see if it has crossbow bolts in its neck."

They flew downriver, rose up over the high timbered ridge that jutted out toward the river below the Moon Creek divide, and found the dead sivilin. There were mawls sitting around in the treetops, and a few soaring above the forest. The sivilin was laying in deep forest just where they had seen the mawls soaring a week earlier. The carcass was partially decomposed and its bloated body made it look even more gigantic than it really was.

Arak used a long obsidian knife to quickly remove three crossbow bolts from its neck and throat area. They were all quad bladed points. It was the same sivilin they'd wounded and left in the forest about two weeks before. They even found the clearing and the tree where they'd flown up and had hidden from the second one that had been chasing them.

They checked four other carcasses that day and found two or three quad bladed arrows in the neck of each one. It appeared as if the sivilin had all clawed at their necks and the quad bladed arrows had caused severe damage. The knife blades they'd inserted through the shafts had cut and caused some of the main arteries or veins to rupture. Most of the arrows were broken or ruined, but they salvaged a few for future use, and most of the points and obsidian blades were intact.

"We've been killing a lot of sivilin." Said Shandra after they'd examined the last one. "At least a dozen I'd say"

Arak and Saran laughed. Arak held up a bloody arrow with pieces of meat hanging off of it. He'd just cut it out of the fourth sivilin's neck. "We can check some more tomorrow if you want, but I think they will all have our arrows in them. They're not dying from disease. We are killing them. Phew they stink worse after they are dead for a week."

"You know we are going to have to convey some images or memories of our hunts to Orem, and show him these arrows." Shandra had her nose pinched as usual whenever she was around one of the dead creatures and she sounded funny as always.

"We'll show Orem first." Said Arak. "He can decide what to tell Duroon or Savant. Magahila will be furious but she's so stern in her old fashioned ways that most everyone thinks she's ridiculous anyway. Orem will outrank her, and Duroon is already suspicious. I think he knows we've tried our luck at dropping on at least a few sivilin."

"We actually showed Orem the images of the first one." Said Shandra. She took the arrow Arak handed her and examined it closely. "Yes this is one of mine. Duroon looked at me when we came in late one night. I think it was a little over a week ago. He asked me how the weather was over the Desowan. He knows we've been out there."

Mace and his sivilin hunters from Taro dropped on one of the flying scourge that day and put a few arrows into it. The thing chased them most of the way down, but then flew up the canyon between Froze to Death and Thunder Mountain and disappeared.

That evening the trio went to Orem's cooking fire and sat on some ancient greasewood chairs that he'd taken out of his walled cliff dwelling. He looked old and tired, and his greying hair was unkempt. He was resting but seemed glad to have some company. Even Shilo came out and sat with them.

"What can I do for you youngsters?" He asked. "Allie has been over and brought food and cakes for us. Both her and Savant were finally able to glide out of the cavern today."

Arak handed him one of the arrows that he'd cut out of a sivilin's neck. "We've been killing sivilin." He said.

Shilo had to stifle an exclamation of awe. "What is that thing?" She asked.

"Hmmm." Orem took the bloody broken arrow; turned it over and examined the knife blades. "I have only seen one like this. The one your grandfather gave you in The Glass Canyon. I thought it was a ceremonial point. You think you have killed a sivilin with this arrow?"

"Lots of them." Said Shandra. "We have been diving on them for weeks. Today we examined four dead carcasses, and they all had our arrows in their necks."

"My imaging skills are almost completely gone." The old leader from The Glass Canyon colony was very attentive now. "I was wondering why you were all so beat up." He pointed at Saran's arm. "That scratch looks almost deep enough for stitches."

Shilo remained completely silent, wide eyed; knowing that she was witnessing something very unusual, maybe heroic, and she didn't want to cause a commotion.

Saran laughed. "It's nothing. After we dive on them and shoot our arrows we hide in the trees. Sometimes they follow us into the forest and we have to fly up through the upper branches to escape just like you taught us years ago."

"Well I'm glad the hunters from Taro are here now." He was grinning from ear to ear. "You can stay safe and start helping out around the city. When we all get our full imaging capabilities back we will be able to see all of your attacks at a gathering." Orem coughed for a moment and took a sip of water. "That was an excellent idea to fix up the old lookout tower. I've walked around up there a few times and wondered how long it's been there."

"Arak found another one of these old quad arrows in the shelter with the knife blade through the shaft when we cleaned out the floor." Said Shandra. "We have found them to be more accurate in the wind when dropping in front of a target or a sivilin. They don't veer off at all like the flat bladed arrows."

Orem still had the crossbow bolt that Arak had given him and he handed it back. "We will have to share this information with the rest of the hunters. I'll make sure you three get some kind of recognition and maybe some privileges of some kind at the academy."

He laughed loud enough to gain attention from anyone nearby, then began coughing uncontrollably while still laughing.

"Try to stay away from the Taro hunters." He said. "And give one of those arrows to Numak. I think he will be able to hunt again in a week or so. Tell him what you've been doing, and please don't do any more sivilin hunting. If any of you get hurt or killed there will be serious consequences."

"Ok" Arak was relieved. He hadn't been sure what kind of repercussions he would encounter when the hunting experiences by the students were out in the open. He was actually responsible for the safety of Saran and Shandra. If anything would have happened to either of them he would probably have been severely punished, and the regret he would have sustained for the rest of his life would have been much worse than any punishment anyway.

They ferried wood that morning and checked on their friends. There were no more deaths due to the strange virus and everyone slowly seemed to be getting better; even the elders. The trio met with Numak that afternoon and explained to him what they'd been doing and showed him the arrows. At first he was skeptical and thought the three students were playing a joke on him. No one could send him good enough telepathic images due to the strange disease, and he couldn't receive them anyway, but when Orem was summoned Numak quickly changed his mind and said he would begin modifying some crossbows and arrows.

The next morning started out about the same as the previous. Seven more sivilin hunters had arrived early that morning and were sleeping in the visitor antechambers of the main cavern. Mace and his group held a meeting with all of the elders and leaders that could attend. Mace had been hearing rumors of students hunting sivilin and he confronted Arak, Shandra, and Saran as soon as the breakfast meeting ended.

The three students had already eaten at the schooling cavern and were sitting at a fire near Orem's dwelling. Mace walked over with an air of authority and nodded a greeting to Orem. "Are you students really thinking of hunting sivilin?" He asked while laughing. "Someone said you have already shot at some."

"Well there was no one else around." Answered Arak. "We had no choice. Everyone was sick; I guess all of the Sagitarian sivilin hunters are still sick."

The rest of Mace's group stood behind him now and some of them began laughing until Orem stood and frowned at them.

Mace looked at Orem and frowned back. "Hmmm. Well you had better keep these three students out of the sky from now on unless they are getting wood or hunting miktas. They're lucky to still be alive." He didn't say anything else. He whipped his crossbow around on the sling as if checking it and strode off.

The three of them were angered as was Orem, but they knew that someday they would get their imaging powers back and then they would be able to show everyone what they'd accomplished.

They all left for the academy so they could help Nooney organize everyone. Magahila was finally up and about, and she had already heard the rumors of the students hunting sivilin. She knew Arak, Shandra, and Saran were just about the only students from the graduating class that hadn't contracted the virus.

Arak and Shandra sat beside Nooney at Magahila's table. They were glad to see her out of bed, but a little worried about breaking rules.

Magahila surveyed them for a moment as she sliced a small stack of honey laced lystocakes coated with thick creamy chalow milk. Her gaze settled on Arak.

"Word is out that you have been falling in front of sivilin." She had a serious look on her face, and her grey streaked hair and yellow eyes made her look very formidable. "That is punishable for many reasons. There will be consequences when this epidemic is over. Whoever is responsible will be severely punished."

Arak just looked at her, but Shandra spoke. "We were never in any danger really. We were very careful."

Magahila coughed and scrutinized them. "How many?"

Arak looked at her and speared a sausage patty off of a platter that one of the younger students brought by. He could tell by her tone that she was very angry; furious. "We're not sure." He said. "We will have to wait until we can project clear images again."

"Well stay out of the sky if you see any more, and if you get wood or look for miktas stay down low in the canyon. Don't go near the sivilin hunters."

Magahila looked at Nooney. "We'll discuss their punishment when the epidemic is resolved."

Nooney nodded at her and waited a moment before answering. "The chalow herds can be rounded up now that there are sivilin hunters present."

They discussed other trivial chores and tasks that were being neglected then Nooney picked three flyers from one of the younger classes and gave them their instructions. Myra, Shek, and Romel flew out of the academy immediately and banked toward the steppes happy not to have to carry wood for a change. The rest just went about their usual tasks. Arak and Shandra decided to hunt south of Sagitar since the new sivilin hunters had seen some wild game in this direction, and they headed for Pyramid mountain.

CHAPTER TWELVE

Cin had taken his time crossing the Desowan. He passed by many landmarks and even places that he'd hidden in past years after dropping and shooting at sivilin. There were more of the flying reptiles in the wasteland now. He'd been seeing two or three almost daily. He began flying at night to elude them, or very early in the morning when storm convection and lightning was also at its minimum. It took him eight nights and three days to cross the Desowan due to the unsettled summer weather.

He tried to send neural signals to anyone that might be searching the wave rifts, but there was nothing. The neural rifts were strangely silent, and he knew Miz or Arak would be searching for him. They would never give up. Cin had always been able to home in on a signal from someone in the Desowan when he was hunting, but there was no one, and this worried him. He'd been gone for over three months, and he knew something was wrong. There should be sivilin hunters out over the Desowan.

Whenever there was a broken cloud ceiling during the day he would stay above for fear of being attacked again. He was able to make it to the last three deep canyons and their intermittent waterways and lakes before anything unusual occurred. He had just finished an afternoon nap and a dinner of smoked jerky when a sivilin surprised him after dark. He flew next to a high mesa gaining altitude and the thing had been sitting on the edge of the cliff. Cin had flown past without noticing the creature and it attacked him almost instantly. He had to dive quickly to the base of the mesa and change direction. He was able to fly around the side of the huge rocky projection and hide amongst some boulders in a khiska thicket. Luckily the sivilin flew around the side of the mesa in the gloom and it continued on past his hiding place.

Cin soared onward with the upper air flow at night and just took his time crossing the dangerous wasteland. He rose to timberline and a half one morning and was finally able to see the mountain range. Mount Sagitar and Thunder were clearly visible about a hundred miles to the west. He soared effortlessly with the upper westward flow for a couple more hours without sighting any sivilin, but then as he neared the mountains he was shocked to see at least four or five of them climbing up over the pass between Sagitar and Thunder. He was too far away to discern if there were any hunters anywhere, and when he tried to send or receive a neural signal he was unsuccessful.

Cin followed the sivilin up over the pass awhile later and looked down into the canyon. He could see five sivilin far below now, and he was very relieved to see that they were finally being attacked by hunters. One of them was out in front and was chasing several hunters in a steep dive. Two of the other sivilin were following, but one was flying up the canyon past the cliffs below Thunder mountain as if unconcerned. The fifth suddenly took a completely different tangent, and started a disturbing dive toward the chalow steppes.

Arak and Shandra were coming around the side of Pyramid mountain after a short southern hunting expedition when Arak noticed the sivilin. They were almost to the ground and there were a lot of them. He pointed, but Shandra had already seen them.

"Hurry!" He shouted. "They might need some help!" The two youngsters flew as fast as they could up the canyon heedless of Magahilas warning. There were sivilin going in every direction it seemed, and all of the sivilin hunters appeared to have dropped into the trees already. A sivilin was rising from the steppes coming directly toward them with something in its talons. Arak could see that it was not a chalow and he was very disturbed. It was one of the young students.

He continued onward straight toward the sivilin and when he caught a nice updraft along the side of Pyramid mountain he began circling tightly. In just a few minutes he was above timberline. He stayed within the thermal while watching the sivilin. It had also caught an updraft and was circling above the steppes now.

Shandra was still close behind Arak when he banked to the north. He was at least two thousand feet above the sivilin now and about a mile from it. He kept closing the distance and climbing to make sure he stayed above the huge flying lizard. It was a giant with a wingspan of at least a hundred and twenty feet and it was carrying its prey loosely as if unconcerned. The old behemoth's wings were scarred and torn; probably from past aerial battles with its own kind, and its hide was also scarred and sunbleached in places. The right wing had a triangular slice missing and Arak realized that there was definitly something familiar about the creature. It looked like the same one that had chased them to the treehouse but he couldn't be sure.

Arak could tell that the young klute in the sivilin's front talons was either unconscious or dead as he continued to close the gap. When he was about three hundred yards above the creature he began circling in cadence. They were in the same thermal now. Arak slowly closed in on the sivilin until he was directly above and behind.

Shandra was a quarter mile from him and safely out of harm when he dropped on the sivilin. Arak flew right in behind and above the flying beast. He was between the sivilin's wings and only about twenty yards behind the thing's head when he aimed carefully, allowed for wind resistance, and pulled the trigger. The crossbow bolt struck the sivilin right at the base of the skull and it suddenly stiffened and began to roll over on its side with one wing folded backward. There was no noise as was the case when shooting one of them in the throat. Suddenly it just went completely limp and began to tumble toward the rocky canyon below.

Arak could see the body of the young female as she was flung from the talons with centrifugal force created by the sivilin's sudden barrel roll, and he dove as fast as he could. She was tumbling out of control above the sivilin and he finally grabbed her around her tiny waist. He recognized her as Myra and knew she was eight or nine years old. She was bleeding in places, but he couldn't see any life threatening injuries. He was almost sure that she was still alive and unconscious. Her wing span was only about ten feet but he still had trouble sustaining flight with her wings waving and swinging in his way. He finally maintained a glide about twenty five hundred feet above the ground and stabilized it toward Froze to Death mountain.

When he looked down he couldn't believe what he was seeing. There were at least thirty klutes standing just outside of the main cavern, and they were all watching the drama that was unfolding within the canyon. They were directly below him. The giant sivilin he'd just shot in the back of the head was somersaulting over and over and falling directly toward them.

Duroon had heard a racket out in the canyon so he'd gone to the mouth of the main cavern and peered upward toward Thunder mountain. He could see the sivilin hunters plummeting toward the forest north of Sagitar with at least three sivilin following. The shrieking was loud as the angry monsters chased the hunters, and he knew one was wounded. Soon at least twenty of the inhabitants that were able to move about and glide had walked down the stairway and were standing beside him watching the action from between the planted fruit bushes in the gardens near the cave entrance.

The three sivilin had already disappeared over the timbered ridge between Froze to Death and Thunder mountain, but the noise had alerted the whole cavern and more and more spectators were coming out to see what was going on. Dozens stood on the parapet in the cavern below the overhanging ceiling including Magahila and Orem.

Suddenly something alerted a few of the audience members; perhaps a shadow beyond the turquoise stream in the center of the small canyon, or a noise above. Someone pointed straight up and began yelling.

"Get back! Its falling out of the sky!"

Everyone began running toward the overhanging cliff wall that housed the main cavern and it wasn't a bit too soon. The dead sivilin plowed face first into the rock strewn canyon next to the carefully groomed gardens less than hundred and fifty yards from the cave mouth seconds later.

Arak made a wide gliding turn and followed it down. He stumbled and fell when he touched down but Myra was still in his arms.

Duroon was having trouble comprehending what had just transpired, and it took him a moment to jump into action. He dodged his way between eight or ten foot tall fruit trees toward Arak and knelt down beside Myra. A few seconds later Shandra touched down about fifteen feet from them.

Myra's head was bloody and she had a deep gash in her side but she was breathing. They carried her up the staircase into the cavern and she regained consciousness while they were cleansing her wounds. For some reason the sivilin hadn't ripped her to shreds as was the usual case with the species, but she had a long dangerous life threatening cut across her ribs and a gash on her forehead. Both cuts would have to be sewn shut, and Duroon sent for brandy and tiral root to ease the young student's pain before retrieving his suturing supplies. Her wings were torn and ripped in three places, but luckily none of the thin flexible bones were broken, and they would regenerate and heal.

Most everyone had followed Duroon up the staircase, but there were a few stragglers looking at the dead sivilin. Arak stood and walked to the stairs. Some of them had never seen one up close; just images or skulls hanging on the wall. Suddenly there was someone familiar standing on top of the carcass as if examining it. Arak was dumfounded to see his father.

That evening there was a celebration of sorts in the main cavern. Klutes that were strong enough all gathered around and some even played their musical instruments. A few of them could send and receive images, but just fuzzy memories as if out of focus.

Mace's group had succeeded in killing a sivilin, and of course there was one laying out in front of the main cave stinking up the whole area. Nobody seemed to mind the stench yet, not even one of the gardeners that had shrugged off the illness. They did realize that the thing would have to be cut into pieces and hauled away soon as the wind was not always cooperative and sometimes the stench would permeate the whole inside of the main cavern.

As the weeks passed everyone began regaining their imaging skills. Several holidays had been missed due to the pandemic so all of the klute colonies deemed that there should be an image sharing in Sagitar on the night of the next full moon. The red moon; or zinda hunter would be about three quarters at the same time and it would be the brightest evening for some time.

All of the sivilin hunters had switched over to quad bladed arrows and the sivilin were slowly being pushed back. Only a few a week were coming over the mountains by the time autumn came for its yearly visit. The elders and supreme leaders of all of the klute colonies had decided that only neck shots should be ventured. Flying up between the wings of a sivilin and shooting one in the back of the head had been judged as far too dangerous.

Cin had finally recovered from the virus, and he was just getting so he could project images to his full capability when Sagitar began receiving hundreds of guests for the huge celebration. Not everyone had survived the sickness, but most had.

The leaves had turned their colors, and Miz had been busy for a couple of weeks gathering rare wild ripened autumn fruits and berries so she could brew a few of her famous wines and brandies. The weather cooperated on the first night of the image sharing and more than two thousand klutes were present in the Sagitarian glacial cirque when Cin projected his thoughts of the continent beyond the arctic sea. It was the largest gathering of the race in decades.

Arak and Shandra snuck some wine and they enjoyed seeing Cin's images again. They both hoped and knew that someday they would probably be able to visit the strange place and its new found dangers.

Arak, Shandra, and Saran had dropped on twenty eight sivilin, and nineteen carcasses had been found in the nearby canyons and on the slopes leading down into the Desowan. All nineteen of them had quad bladed arrows in their necks. One of them had probably been killed by Arak, Enneka and Shandra before Enneka had come down with the virus. The twentieth had been shot in the back of the head. Sivilin meat had been known to cause neurological problems in the klute race in the past so the stinking carcass had been cut into pieces and thrown into the river.

Arak was summoned to the huge granite rostrum after his father had shared his images of the arctic and the continent beyond. The small pack of flying lizards had interested everyone, but the cave pictographs had been the main focus of attention, and of course the huge valley along the east coast that seemed to be full of sivilin.

Shandra, Saran, and Enneka accompanied Arak to the rostrum and they climbed the stairway. They would now share neural images of their sivilin kills to the extra large crowd.

Silence usually reigned during an imaging ceremony. It was deemed impolite to speak or break the silence in any manner while images were being shared or even after they were shared for at least a few minutes. Arak and his three friends gazed out at the huge crowd in the bright moonlight and suddenly someone yelled.

"Hail the sivilin hunters!"

In a glacial cirque, on a distant planet forty thousand light years from earth, the silence at a telepathic image sharing was suddenly broken by twenty five hundred klutes who began cheering the most dangerous sivilin hunters to fly in the skies over Sagitar for centuries.

Made in the USA
San Bernardino, CA
07 December 2017